To Live & Die
In
Chiraq

Y. Blak Moore

ADULT NOVELS ALSO BY Y. BLAK MOORE

In My Brother's Footsteps
Heartless
Diesel Dolls
Triple Take2: Champagne's Kiss
Triple Take
The Apostles
Slipping

DEDICATION

Dedicated to Ytteb Martin of Y Martin Editing, my Sister Dear and the only person that has been with me through every level of my writing career. Thank you so much for the big and small.

Love and Light beautiful Tebby.

First printing: 2020
ISBN 9781734907001
R & M Publishing
Chicago, Illinois 60628

Ordering information:
Special discounts are available on quantity purchases by corporations, associations, educators, and others. For details contact the publisher.

U.S. trade bookstores and wholesalers: Please contact R & M Publishing
Tel: (312)650-9720 or rhuemoorebooks@gmail.com

Book Editing/Layout/Cover Design by Y Martin Editing at ymartinediting@gmail.com

CHAPTER 1

Tureon "Tutu" Young walked out of the kitchen carrying a freshly microwaved bowl of Ramen noodles and a large McDonald's cup full of red Kool-aid. He walked down the short hallway to the living room and deposited himself on the couch. He placed his cup on the end table and ate a forkful of noodles. He put the bowl down and scampered to the kitchen. The sound of a kitchen cabinet could be heard slamming and seconds later he regained his seat with a bottle of hot sauce. After several healthy squirts of hot sauce Tutu tasted his noodles again, this time nodding his head in approval.

He sat the bowl of noodles on the coffee table and took a big gulp of his Kool-aid before picking up the video game controller to play his game. In between slurping mouthfuls of noodles, he played his game. Soon though he grew bored of playing the game alone and decided to text his older brother, Tyrese.

Tutu: wya

Tyrese: y

Tutu: Stop playn boi wya

Tyrese: lol u aint my daddy

Tutu: yo daddy aint yo daddy

Tyrese: lmao we got the same daddy stupid

Tutu: stop capn when u comin home

Tyrese: omw

Tutu: gang with u

Tyrese: y

Tutu: so I can kik they butt n 2k tired of beatn u

Tyrese: u can only beat me wit lebron

Tutu: u can pik who I play wit

Tutu: how long

Tyrese: u thirsty I'm walkn that way now

Tutu: stop lyin

Tyrese: come on the porch

Tutu leapt from the couch and ran out of their first floor apartment onto the porch in his socks. At the opposite end of the street his brother and two of his friends were crossing the street onto the block. The two-flat building they lived in with their mother was closer to the north end of the block, and Tyrese was approaching from the south. A wide grin broke out on his face when he saw his brother.

"Come on y'all!" yelled Tutu. "Don't get scared now."

Tyrese and his friends laughed and pointed at Tutu as they continued toward the building. Behind them an older model, silver Toyota Camry with tinted windows hesitated in the intersection, before it made a right turn onto Gray Street. As the car crept along slowly the sun glinted off the metallic silver of the paintjob making it catch Tutu's eye. With a smile still on his face, Tutu turned to look at the vehicle as it glided slowly up the street. As it drew parallel to his brother and friends, Tutu noticed the dark tinted windows on the car slide down out of the way. Two handguns were extended out of the car on the passenger side, the pistol in the front had a long, wicked looking clip protruding from it, and the rear passenger had a large chrome revolver that seemed to sparkle in the sun.

Tutu's eyes grew huge and round as he immediately recognized the danger his brother and friends were in. He wanted to yell out to his brother to run, to take cover, to get down, but fear froze his vocal chords as his mouth opened wide, but not a single word came out of it.

By that time Tyrese, Danno and Price were close enough to see the look of shock and fear on Tutu's face, though they were still four buildings away from him. Tyrese was still smiling thinking his little brother was playing with them as he turned his head to follow Tutu's shocked gaze. He fully expected nothing to be behind them, but instead the smile melted from his face as he saw the silver sedan with guns hanging out the windows.

Tyrese's mouth fell open, and then he managed to blurt out, "Run y'all they got poles!" Someone in the vehicle yelled, "8 Deuce Hotheads, GSG killers!" a millisecond before both guns roared to life. The staccato of the nine millimeter mixed with the roaring of the magnum almost sounded like a deadly drum solo.

Tutu had often heard people describing moments like this by saying everything slowed way down, but to him everything sped up to an insane pace. All he had time to do was sit down hard on his butt to take cover behind the brick porch.

On the sidewalk, Danno sprinted into a gangway and with one arm covering his face he shot back at their attackers several times before his gun jammed.

He stooped on one knee quickly to try and free the jam, but the flying bullets were pelting the walls near him so he turned and fled through the gangway.

Tyrese and Price weren't as lucky as a volley of shots hit them. Price took several bullets before he managed to dive behind a short brick wall circling the building's property. After shouting out the warning, Tyrese tried to run, but only made it three or four steps before he was mowed down by a deadly hail of lead. His lifeless body wobbled as he took his last step and he pitched face first onto a grassless patch of dirt. Several more shots aimed at him either hit the dirt or passed over his body as he lay there.

From the cover of the porch all Tutu could do was watch in horror as his brother was gunned down. It seemed like an eternity before the shooters pulled their guns into the car and sped off, blowing through the stop sign at the corner. The driver made a right on the next street and the car that had brought death to their block was gone just like that. As the car made its getaway, Tutu ran to Tyrese as fast as his socked feet would carry him. The closer he got, he could see two gaping holes in his brother's back and his blood had already begun to blacken the dirt around his torso. He fell to his knees in the dirt beside Tyrese and rolled him over onto his back, which was hard because his hands were slick with blood. He pulled and tugged barely able to see through the river of tears on his face, and eventually managed to turn Tyrese. Tyrese's light gray hoodie had three bullet holes in it, and was now maroon with blood on the chest and side area. Tutu had never seen death up close and personal before, but he knew from the lifeless look in his brother's wide open eyes that he was a long way away from here.

Price had come from behind the brick wall that had probably saved his life, and limped over to look at his dead friend. He was wincing from the dripping holes in his arm and leg, as his tears began to free themselves from his eyes. He turned away and went to sit on the steps of the closest building. Danno came walking back out of the gangway with his useless firearm dangling in his hand. He was crying and shaking his head in disbelief as he looked down at his oldest friend in the world. He knelt in the bloody dirt beside Tutu and put his arm around his shoulders.

Up and down the block, people began to come out of their houses and apartments to see the aftermath of so many gunshots. They quickly noticed the small group of boys grieving, bleeding and crying. A teenage girl walked near them and shrieked when she noticed it was Tyrese on the ground.

"They done kilt Tyrese y'all!" she yelled, causing a gasp from several of their neighbors.

"Somebody call the police they done shot Tyrese and Price," an elderly man said, "Them peoples is on the way, the fire partment and polices. Just hold on y'all."

A trio of boys came running up the block to the scene at the same time as a late model black foreign car flew around the corner and screeched to a halt scaring everyone. The driver and the passenger got out of the car. They were both carrying guns and walked over to see Tyrese while the crowd watched them warily.

The driver, a slim, dark man with a short curly afro looked down at Tyrese, after a moment he looked away. "Danno, who did this bro?" he asked in a calm, but deadly voice. "Who kilt my lil bro Reese?"

"It was some 8 Deuces, we ain't even see them bro til it was too late, they had already slid up," Danno said miserably.

"My banger jammed Geno, wasn't nothing I could do but get up out that jam. Reese didn't make it and they shot up Price, he should be good though."

"It was 8 Deuces. It was the Hotheads," people in the crowd whispered and repeated to anyone within earshot.

"What they was in?" Geno asked.

"A little silver four door with tints, bro."

Geno looked at the gun in Danno's hand. "Them people finta be pulling up G, you need to get up outta here with that pole."

"On God, I'm staying with my homie," Danno said in a tone that left no room for discussion.

"I'm gone, they smoked one of ours, we gone smoke one of theirs before the day is done," Geno promised.

He and his passenger got into the sedan and burned rubber down the street. In his wake, the crowd grew quickly as the word began to spread to the surrounding blocks. Some of the onlookers even started to jostle one another to get a closer look at Tyrese, one young guy trying to get some video footage with his cell phone even bumped Danno by accident. Danno stood up and snatched his phone and with a mighty heave, he slung it as far down the street as he could. The boy looked like he wanted to say something, but the gun in Danno's hand made him think better of it. Instead he trotted off to see if he could find his phone.

"Don't nobody take no pics or video of my homie or it's bussin," Danno threatened as he glared at the crowd, noticing several people hurry up and tuck their phones away. "I'm dead ass too. I don't care who you is neither, I said what I said."

In the distance the wailing of sirens could be heard as police and emergency vehicles drew nearer. The older man that called the ambulance stepped closer to Danno.

"Young fella, that's the ambulance and cops," he said. "Don't get yourself locked up for nothing."

"Old head mind your business," Danno said, trying to sound fierce, but his voice was choking with his emotion.

The older man said, "I usually do mind my business son, but I know you're not thinking this through. I don't want to see you go to jail or possibly worse. Your friends are gonna need you now more than ever, and it does them no good for you to be sitting in jail."

Danno looked at the older guy through his tears for a moment. "You right old head," he conceded. He leaned down to the sobbing Tutu and said, "I'll be right back Tutu. Right back. I gotta go put this banger up." He stood up and pushed his way through the crowd. "I'll be right back," he said to Price as he headed for the gangway.

On the ground beside his brother's body, covered in blood and dirt, Tutu sobbed as he pulled his cell phone from his pocket and called his mother.

CHAPTER 2

Shameeka "Meeka" Young pulled on the jacket of her navy blue Nike jogging suit making sure she zipped it to where a generous portion of her cleavage still showed. Even though it was her first born son's funeral, she wanted to look extra good, because you never could tell when the opportunity to meet a man would present itself.

It had been awhile since she'd had some male company because she'd been working so hard at her job, but right now she wouldn't say no to some 'comforting' from the right guy. Also, if for some reason her deadbeat baby's father decided to show his no good face at the funeral, she wanted to be looking so fire Tyrone would want to kick himself for running out on her. He also needed to know that she was doing just fine without him. She slid her feet into her new pair of all white, low top Air Force Ones, before looking at her reflection in her dresser mirror as she sprayed on a couple of light blasts of her PINK body spray. She put the bottle down, but decided to give herself one last spritz, so she did.

She returned the bottle to her dresser top and smoothed out an errant hair from her long sew-in.

She turned from side to side in the mirror, admiring the way the jogging suit hugged her body tightly in all the right places.

At first she had been against wearing the jogging suits, but Tureon spoke so passionately about wearing them as a tribute to Tyrese she gave in to his wishes. She knew Tyrese did love those suits with his crispy white Nike Air Force Ones because she'd bought many a pair.

Her cell phone was sitting next to her ashtray overflowing with cigarette butts on top of a storage tote next to her bed. She unplugged it from the charger and looked at the time. It was time to go, so she stuffed her charger into her purse, picked up her sunglasses and put the phone into her jacket pocket. She touched up her lip gloss and smacked her lips several times to make sure it was in place. She dumped the gloss into her purse and slung it over her shoulder. She left her room and went to the living room to retrieve her cigarettes, taking one from the pack and lighting it before she approached the bedroom door of the room her two sons once shared together. First Meeka listened at the door, she could hear some music playing so she knocked lightly before opening it. Her youngest son, Tureon was sitting on his brother's bed brushing his waves. He wore the same Nike jogging suit and shoes as she did. "Tutu, baby it's time to go," Meeka said softly with her cigarette dangling from the corner of her mouth. "The family car will be here any minute and we don't want to be late."

"I'm ready ma," Tutu said as he stood up and gave his hair a few more brush strokes. He put his brush on the dresser, pulled on his fresh New York Yankees snapback hat and followed his mother out the door. They left the apartment, locked the apartment door and went out onto the porch. The limo hadn't arrived yet so he took a seat on the brick porch arms.

It had only been there a week, but he had already grown sick of the makeshift memorial his brother's friends had made down the street on the spot he was killed. It was filled with religious candles, teddy bears, and empty Remy and Hennessy bottles lined up like dead soldiers. The memorial was supposed to be a tribute to Tyrese, but to him it was a constant reminder of that deadly day, as if he needed reminding. Meeka leaned against the wall with her dark sunglasses on her face and impatiently tapped her foot as she smoked her cigarette. She removed her pint of liquor from her purse and took a swig. She replaced the cap on the bottle and returned the Henny to her purse.

"Tutu, I forgot to tell you I talked to your Aunt Vena. She gone be there. Her and your Aunt Kim. Kim sposed to be making her good ass banana pudding for the repast and one for us to take home. She gone make it just how you like it too, with all them strawberries in it too."

"That's good Ma," Tutu said half-heartedly.

Meeka's voice was colder when she said, "Oh yeah, she said that she talked to yo daddy. He out in Joliet but he gone try and make it to the service."

Tutu's laugh was cold and uncaring as he said, "Yeah right, Ma. That dude ain't been there in Reese's life, he shole ain't gone be there in his death."

Long ago, Tutu had stopped believing any message his father sent. Too many Christmases, birthdays and special occasions had passed without so much as a single visit, or card or call from him to ever believe anything his father may have said or promised. Long ago he moved to Joliet with his new family, and in Tutu's opinion it was like he'd moved off the planet. "Forget all that Ma, call them peoples and see where that car at." Meeka took her phone out of her purse, but Tutu said, "That's alright Ma, this is probably them right there."

Sure enough the long, black Cadillac limousine driving up the street, stopped in front of their address, a funeral home employee got out of the car and held the back door open for them. They both walked down the stairs and got in the rear of the car. The employee closed the car door behind them and got back in the front passenger seat. Inside of the limo, Tutu and his mother sat side by side, so close their shoulders were touching even though there was plenty of room. The ride was super smooth and it felt like the limo was gliding as they headed for the funeral home. Soft gospel music leaked from the speakers as they both sat lost in thought content to listen. Meeka lit a cigarette as she nervously tapped her foot.

"Excuse me ma'am," the limo driver said, looking in the rearview mirror at Meeka. "I know this is a hard time that you're going through, but I'm going to have to ask you to put the cigarette out."

Usually she would have given the driver a hard time, but she just didn't have the energy for it right now. She rolled her eyes and took one more pull off of her cigarette before she let the window down and flicked it outside. She took her bottle from her purse and unscrewed the top, holding it up so the driver could see it in the mirror.

"Do you mind if I at least have a little something to sip on?" she asked.

The driver nodded his head. "Go right ahead ma'am. The cigarette thing wasn't personal, that's company policy. If the boss gets in here and smells it, I'm out of a job."

Meeka tipped her bottle to him and took a long swig of the brown liquor. She capped the bottle and returned it to her purse. She sat back with Tutu and listened to the gospel music for the last mile or so of the ride. They arrived at the large funeral home on South Halsted Street with a few minutes to spare before Tyrese's wake was set to start. A greeter ushered them into the chapel and to the front pew with the family. Several cousins had to scoot down or get up entirely so they could sit down next to his mother's twin sister, Shaneeka. Other members of the family were also trickling in to view the body. A heavyset, older lady with bad feet came forward and handed Shameeka and Tureon a large, colorful obituary.

"Ma'am, I suggest you take this time to have a few extra moments with the deceased before the bulk of the crowd arrives," the older woman politely suggested.

Behind her sunglasses, Meeka said sourly, "I done made my peace with my baby and my savior, I'm good. I know Jesus and my boy knew Jesus, so I know that ain't him in that box. He's with my Savior in heaven so ain't no sense doing all that about no body. My baby is always with me in my heart and my Jesus said I'm gone see him again, so y'all gone do what y'all gone do. Tutu, you gone up there and say goodbye to your big brother."

Tutu didn't want to, but his aunt Neeka sitting next

to him grabbed his wrist, and all but dragged him to stand in front of his brother's navy blue casket. Tyrese was wearing the same outfit as them, and his dreads were arranged on the satin coffin pillow. They were shiny and had been groomed perfectly. His New York Yankees cap rested on his chest. Tutu stood there awkwardly trying to look everywhere but at his brother as his aunt put her arm around his shoulders.

"They did a good job on my nephew," Neeka said. "He look just like he sleeping. I wanna tell him to get up he look so full of life."

Tutu looked up at his favorite auntie like she'd lost her mind; to him, his brother's body looked like it had never contained life. For a moment he thought he would be all cried out, but as he thought about how he would never see Tyrese alive again he lost his composure. The thought that he would never wrestle with him, jump out of closets and scare him, play games and watch movies with him, text and call him, get on his nerves, steal his Snickers candy bars out of the freezer, wear his clothes, split gyros with him and argue about Lebron James and Kevin Durant again was just too much for him. Different people patted him on the back, hugged him and told him it would be okay as he bawled loudly.

It took several of them, but finally they managed to get Tutu back to his seat in the first row. Nestled between his aunt and mother, Tutu managed to calm down after a while. Family, friends and Tyrese's gang members had begun viewing the body and they filtered past the front row offering their condolences to the family, hugging his mother and auntie and patting him on the head or back. The majority of the gangbangers wore t-shirts, hoodies and sweatshirts fixed with pictures of Tyrese. Though many of his gang acted respectfully, there were quite a few of them that were loud, noisy and rude. They smelled like weed and liquor, talked and cursed loudly amongst themselves without regard for the family or other funeral-goers, and the usher had to remind many of them to remove their hats.

He couldn't tell through his tears just how many of his brother's friends offered him condolences; he just knew it was a lot of them, so many in fact Tutu lost count. The wake was almost over when a girl he'd seen his brother Facetime, and bring over the crib, came shimmying down the aisle in a dress so tight everyone wondered how she could even breathe in that thing. She was wailing in anguish like her best friend, mother, and puppy had died all at the same time and somehow when she managed to make it to Tyrese's casket she turned the theatrics up even more. His aunt Neeka looked at him questioningly with raised eyebrows, but he just shrugged his shoulders. Tutu looked back into the pew behind them at Quita, the mother of his brother's baby daughter, Tyra, to see what her response would be toward the caterwauling girl. She and Tyrese had called it quits about 6 months ago, and she wasn't letting him see his daughter around the time he died.

Quita got up from her seat and carried Tyra up to the front pew. She sat the happy child on Meeka's lap and said, "Tyra sit right here with yo G-ma, I'll be right back." Quita was all business as she marched over to the girl at Tyrese's casket acting a fool and grabbed a handful of her sew-in. Her grip on the girl's hair immobilized her, and Quita swiftly rattled off a series of punches that landed on the girl's eyes, nose and lips.

Instead of trying to separate the fight's participants, people grabbed their cell phones and started recording the one-sided brawl. Quita drug the stunned girl back up the aisle and out of the chapel, causing her to lose one of her ridiculously tall, high heels. In the lobby, she whacked the girl a few more times in the face for good measure, then slung her to the floor. Using the pants leg of a man standing next to her, the girl pulled herself up to her feet. She wobbled as she pulled down her dress which had hiked itself up around her hips. She kicked her remaining shoe off as she glared at Quita.

Quita shot daggers from her eyes. "You better stop playing with me, before you spend the rest of the day in the emergency room getting patched up."

The girl seemed to be weighing her options as she tried to untangle her hair. One of her extra-long eyelashes was barely hanging on making her seem cross-eyed so she snatched it off. To Quita, she said, "You so petty. I can't believe you even got down like this. Tyrese wasn't even with you. I know because…"

Quita faked at her like she was going to attack again. The girl thought better of it, turned and high-tailed it out of there. She burst through the funeral home doors almost knocking down several people as she fled north on Halsted Street.

A couple of videographers patted Quita on the back and congratulated her as she made her way back inside the chapel. She walked back to the front row as if nothing had happened.

"Meeka, you want me to get her?" Quita asked.

"No she can stay with me," Meeka replied as she snuggled Tyra. "Knowing my son, you might have to do that a couple more times, ain't that right Ty-ty."

Tyra giggled and smiled totally unaware that ten feet away from her, lay her deceased father. Quita returned to her seat in the second row and scanned the proceedings carefully looking for any more disrespectful side chicks. She relaxed a bit as she saw the casket being closed, meaning the funeral was prepared to begin.

As the pastor began the funeral with a prayer, Neeka put her arm around Tutu's shoulders and pulled him close. He didn't resist, leaning against her as he watched and listened to the proceedings. The funeral went along at a surprisingly fast clip and was pretty uneventful, except for a few hiccups like some of his friends cursing, and taking too long during the remarks section.

Just when Tutu thought he would be able to make it to the end of the funeral without breaking down again, one particularly sad musical selection by the female soloist reduced many of them to tears. The younger crowd got up and left the chapel. Through his tears Tutu noticed Danno, Price and some of his brother's other friends leaving out of the chapel too.

"Finta get some air, Auntie," he mumbled as he slid from under her arm.

"Gone head," she said, while fanning herself with the obituary and waving her hand slowly back and forth in the air at the singer.

Tutu walked up the aisle and out of the chapel. Outside the funeral home, he saw for the first time there were more people on the outside than in the actual service. It was more of a party atmosphere out there, with people laughing, joking, drinking and smoking. It was a direct contrast to the gloominess of the chapel. He spotted Danno and the others standing in a crowd and walked over to them.

As soon as he saw Tutu, Danno put his arm around him. "Man, lil bro, I'm gone miss my bro Ty," he lamented. "I been sliding for my bro since the day they pulled it. Nothing but pressure, all day every day. Eight Deuce can't live after killing my guy and that's on God."

"That's right Tutu, we at them day and night," agreed another of Tyrese's friends. "Ain't no more outside for them, and that's on my granny."

His brother's friend Geno leaned in to him. "I got something for you Tutu. We can't have gang out here naked. Check it out."

Tutu stepped closer and Geno pulled a gun from under his hoodie and handed it to him.

"That's a .380 boy," Geno said after hitting the blunt someone handed him. "You can hold it down with that and get yo lick back. If you see any of them 8 Deuces, you bang at they ass. Don't hesitate neither because they ain't gone hesitate to get down on you. Now put that up."

Tutu tucked the gun into his waistband. He stood and listened to the older boys talk as they passed around blunts and sipped their liquor. Instinctively, Tutu reached for a lit blunt when one was passed within arm's reach and took his first hit of weed. Tears of a different sort sprang into his eyes as he choked, coughed and gagged from the weed. A girl took the blunt from him and patted him on the back as she smoked it. When he was finally able to breathe again and straightened up, his eyes were bloodshot red.

"On that car! Watch that car right there!" shouted someone turning everyone's attention to the street. A late model Lexus sedan zoomed past the funeral home and kept going, so everyone stood down from the high alert.

"Little Tyrese, you ready hunh," Danno said proudly as he put the safety back on his gun and tucked it back into his pants. "That's what I'm talking about. Lil bro gone be smoking on his own 8 Deuce in no time, watch."

Tutu was puzzled by Danno's comment until he looked down at his hand, and saw he had pulled his pistol out and was gripping it tightly. Bashfully he tucked his gun away like he'd seen Danno do with his pistol.

Price came forward and extended his middle finger toward him. "GSG," he said looking Tutu in his eyes.

Tutu stepped forward and extended his middle finger also, locking it with Price's finger in their gang handshake.

"8 Deuce killer," Tutu said. "Gray Street Gang."

Danno came forward and shook hands with Tutu. He hugged him tightly as he whispered in his ear, "Tyrese you can rest up my boy, me and Tutu down here on that from this day on. On God."

CHAPTER 3

Tutu sat on the edge of his bed in the early morning quietness staring at his brother Tyrese's bed. On the day Tyrese died, he had laid an outfit out on his bed that he was going to put on later, after he got his haircut and took a shower. He was coming from the barbershop the day he was ambushed by rival gang members and killed. In fact that was one of the theories surrounding his death floating around the neighborhood. It was being said that there may have been someone in that shop that day that was an 8 Deuce that must have dropped his location to the opps. Either that or the opps had been sliding and as they drove around, they noticed Tyrese lacking at the shop.

To Tutu, neither theory mattered, all he knew was that his big brother was dead. He ran his fingers through the makings of a nappy mini afro. His once wavy, well-groomed hair was growing bushy since he hadn't brushed it in over a week. He hadn't done anything to it since his brother's funeral and was seriously considering growing dreads.

After stretching long and loudly he reached under his pillow and pulled out his gun. He took the clip out; it was empty after last night's activities. He went to his closet to retrieve his box of bullets so he could reload his pistol. Since the day his brother was laid to rest, he had been opp shopping with Danno three times. The first time he didn't get a shot off it happened so fast. One minute they were walking, and the next moment Danno was blasting at a fleeing boy. The next time he managed to get a few shots off, succeeding only in murdering the wall he kept hitting, but last night they spotted a carful of 8 Deuces at the McDonald's on 69th and State. He and Danno were both in Geno's car riding around looking for 8 Deuces when they saw them. Geno swung around the block, but the black Altima they were looking for had pulled out of the parking lot and was headed south. They followed the black car for two blocks looking for an opportunity to pull alongside them to shoot at them.

The car in front of them drove onto the Dan Ryan expressway at the 71st Street entrance ramp. Geno followed them without hesitation. He told them he was going to pull alongside the 8 Deuces in the car ahead of them and when they were parallel he expected them to shoot. Tutu looked at Danno and he seemed ready to act, so he prepared himself. Close to 75th Street, Geno whipped his car around to the driver's side of the Altima and pulled alongside it. He let the passenger windows down and both Danno and Tutu extended their weapons. Danno started firing at the sedan and Tureon followed suit as they both sprayed the car with bullets. The driver of the black Nissan swerved toward the shoulder of the road and crashed into the wall.

Geno sped up and exited the expressway via the ramp on 79th Street and drove west like nothing had happened. They rode around for a bit longer, smoking weed and talking excitedly about the shooting. Both older boys admired the way he took care of his business and that made him feel proud.

By the time Geno dropped him off at home, Tutu was so high all he could do was smile and giggle. He keyed his way into the apartment, walked past his mother passed out drunk on the couch and went to his room. He pulled off his clothes, tucked his pistol under his pillow and passed out, too.

Now that it was morning and he was sober, he didn't know how he felt about what he'd done last night. He turned on the television and saw that two people were hit in the car he'd help shoot up last night, and one of them didn't make it. He figured that he was supposed to be happy about getting some payback for his brother's murder, but he didn't feel any relief. The misery of Tyrese being gone still remained. The lump in his chest he'd had ever since that awful day was still there, sitting like a brick in his chest.

Also, he had to deal with the fact that at the ripe old age of 15 he had just helped to shoot and kill someone. And the scary fact was he knew he could and would pull the trigger as many times as need be to make this heartache go away. Geno told him that the more he did it, the easier it would become. He also said that he'd been doing it for so long, he didn't know any other way, but to be a savage. He said he stopped caring a long time ago. When somebody shot his little sister trying to kill a guy that ran through a crowded playground to get away from his assailant, he became heartless. His little sister had snuck to the park that day, and she never made it back home.

While they were riding, Tutu was glad they didn't talk much about Tyrese, mainly because he didn't trust himself not to start crying. Even his mother only mentioned Tyrese absentmindedly. When she realized what she did she would often get sad and start drinking even more. He knew as much as he missed his brother, she had to miss him even more. He had caught her more than once staring at his pictures on Facebook and Instagram.

At first when Tyrese got killed their apartment never seemed to be empty. Family and friends dropped by everyday with chicken, cake and soul food. Their cell phones rang constantly and their online pages were overflowing with people's well wishes and condolences. Weed and alcohol were plentiful too as everybody drank and smoked until the early morning hours almost every day until the funeral. The day after the funeral was a direct contrast; nobody came by the house. Not one single, solitary person. No calls, texts or Facebook posts. There was plenty of alcohol and food left after the repast, but that was it. No one wanted to talk, or look at baby pictures or tell funny stories about Tyrese getting caught up by girls, or how good he was at playing baseball. It just felt like no one cared after they put the dirt on Tyrese's casket.

Those thoughts were making Tutu even more depressed, so he picked his pants up off the floor. He fished a half of a blunt out of his pocket that he'd saved from last night. With his lighter in hand, he slipped on his Nike slides and went to the bathroom. He turned on the shower to use the steam to mask the smell of the marijuana. After he was through smoking he opened the window and went ahead and took a shower.

Wearing only a towel he went back to his room. He sat on the bed and turned on his television. Aimlessly he flicked through the channels for a bit, as usual, there was nothing on. Momentarily he thought about turning on his video game, but he hadn't been able to bring himself to power it up, because it reminded him of Tyrese too much.

He was undecided what to do as he pulled on clean underwear and socks, and in the spur of the moment he put on his school uniform. It had been more than two weeks since he'd been to classes and for the first time in his life he was so bored he decided to go to school. The more he thought about it he actually began to grow a bit excited as he thought of kicking it with his friends, checking out a THOT or two and trying to get them to go, and even possibly making it to most of his classes.

His mind was made up, so he finished dressing and went to the kitchen to get a Pop-Tart before he left for school. His mother was sitting at the kitchen table drinking a cup of coffee in her hotel housekeeper's uniform.

"Hey, Ma," he said as he took the box of toaster pastries from off the top of the refrigerator. He took a pack out of the box, tore it open with his teeth and put the two pastries in the toaster, pushing down the bar to toast them.

"Hey, Tutu," Meeka said, stopping to cough. She poured more cream into her coffee before asking, "So you ready to go back to school? You sure? Cause you know you can stay out a few more days if you want to."

"I'm good, Ma," Tureon said. "It's time. I ain't trying to fail my sophomore year." His Pop-Tarts popped up and he tossed them on a paper plate. "See you later, OG."

Meeka stood up holding her coffee cup and stabbed out her cigarette in the ashtray. "I got to get a move on myself 'fore I miss my train. Have a good day Tutu and be careful."

Carrying his breakfast, Tutu took his clear school book bag from a hook in the front closet and slipped his arms through the straps. In between bites of his hot Pop-Tarts, he left out of the apartment and locked the door behind himself. Outside on the sidewalk he took care not to look at the "spot", though most of his brother's memorial had been removed one early morning by the city. He still walked fast whenever he had to pass it though.

On the way to the bus line he had to walk past his old grammar school. His 8th grade graduating class was the last one the building had seen because it had been closed and scheduled for demolition for over a year now. As a tribute to his brother, one of his gang members had taken neon orange spray paint and written Rest In Peace to Tyrese all over the walls. There was also a list of deceased 8 Deuce Hotheads on the wall with Rest In Piss emblazoned over their names. His chest swelled with pride at seeing the tribute to his big brother.

As he walked along, he had to admit he felt a bit naked without his gun, but he knew the security at school was super tight and he didn't want to chance getting caught with his banger. The bus stop was on the next block and his school was a straight shot from there, so he figured he'd be reasonably safe.

At the bus stop there were a few kids from his school

waiting on the bus too, but none that he knew too well. One boy kept looking at him and Tutu returned his stare, wondering what he was on until the boy threw up the Gray Street Gang sign; he returned his salute.

"Sorry about your brother, bro," the boy said, offering his condolences.

"Thanks, homie" Tutu said a bit awkwardly. He pulled his headphones out of his pocket, connected them to his phone and put the buds in his ears. He began to bob his head like he was listening to music though he wasn't so he wouldn't have to talk to anyone. The CTA bus pulled up to their stop and Tutu boarded it. Several other students on the bus nodded or spoke as he walked past them. He found an empty seat and sat down, putting his book bag in the seat next to him so nobody would sit there. The ride to school was only two miles and he spent that time staring out the window watching the city.

The bus pulled up in front of the school and Tutu disembarked with the rest of the students. On the sidewalk, he took his phone from his pocket to see the time. First period would be starting soon, but he had no intention of attending that class.

Directly across the street was a park with a concrete basketball court. Though he and his friends weren't the best hoopers, they stayed on the court when they didn't have classes and often when they did, hacking one another and shooting bricks. Today was no different as he spotted his homies as he crossed the street to the park. His friends, Varshawn "Vah" Till, Forest "Tree" Pittman, Conray "Con" Tremont and Jordan "Air" Staples were on the court playing what looked like a wild game of varsity. They were so engrossed in their hack fest that they didn't notice him standing on the sidelines for a few moments.

When they did though, they ran and skipped over to him to shake his hand and show him some love. They were all Gray Street affiliates so they knew the handshake.

"Tutu, what you doing back?" Vah asked breathlessly.

Tutu shrugged. "It got boring as hell at the crib."

"I don't know what's wrong with you 'cause if I didn't have to be here, I wouldn't," Tree said.

"Dumb as you is, you need to always be in school," Con joked. "Boy, you don't need no days off. Not even Christmas vacation."

They all laughed, except Tree as he punched Con in the arm, which sparked a round of roughhousing between the two boys while the rest of them watched. Soon enough both boys were winded and were merely circling one another without engaging.

"Y'all through?" Air asked.

"Tutu, what you been on, bro?

"Just chilling and drilling," Tutu answered matter-of-factly.

"That's wassup, that's what I wanna be on," Con said enviously. "I want some of that action."

"We been sliding on a regular, almost every day," Tutu bragged. "Ain't no outside for them lames."

"On God," Con said as he shook up with Tutu. "On Tyrese, 8 Deuce can't live no more."

"That's on gang," Tre said as he shook it up with Con and Tutu.

As they continued to talk amongst themselves, one of the boys still on the court yelled over to them, "Aye y'all we got five, let's run one. What y'all wanna do?"

"We can run a game," Vah shouted back, accepting the challenge. To his friends, he said, "C'mon y'all. Let's whup these bums real quick. I'm trying to go to 3rd period. And don't be gunning neither, Tutu."

"Shut up boy," Tutu said with a grin. "Somebody got to put the ball in the basket, you busters shole don't."

They walked over to the free throw line so they could shoot for first ball. While they were shooting, Tutu put his book bag with his friends' belongings. The other team won first ball and inbounded it to one of their players starting the game. The lead went back and forth as both teams were pretty evenly matched.

During the game, four boys wearing their school uniforms that Tutu didn't recognize, walked up and stopped on the sidelines to watch them play. It seemed that whenever Tureon and his team missed a shot the newcomers laughed extra loud and hard. They also seemed to be cheering on the other team by clapping and shouting when they made a shot. This continued on until a boy on the other team called travelling on Con.

While they were arguing about the validity of the call, one of the boys on the sideline, the one that had been making the most noise, ran over and snatched the ball out of Con's hands. He ran down to the other end of the court and shot a few layups. The boy's friends joined him and took turns rebounding and shooting, while the participants of the game argued back and forth. They finally decided that Con and the boy that made the call would shoot from the 3-point line, whoever hit the shot first it was their team's ball.

"Yo, we need that ball," Con called out to the boys.

They ignored his request and kept shooting around.

"Aye boy, we need that ball," Vah said much louder.

Still the boys ignored them and kept playing with the ball.

"What the...?" Tutu said. "What's wrong with them? They act like they done lost they minds. Who is homie and nem?"

"I think them some of the kids from Montgomery on 81ˢᵗ," Tree speculated. "They school just closed and some of them got sent here."

"They must don't know where they at, they tripping," Air said. "C'mon."

They walked to the other end of the court, where the boys were playing with their game ball. As they got closer, Tutu said, "I don't know what y'all on, but we gone need that rock, we playing with it."

"Y'all was playing with it," said the boy that had taken the ball from Con in the first place. "It looked like y'all was done so we got it now. Y'all can get it back when we done."

"Boy who you think you talking to?" Tutu said. "Y'all better give us that ball before it be a situation."

The boy with the ball smiled.

"Ain't nothing funny, boy," Vah said menacingly. "You bout to get beat up about a ball ain't even yours."

"Y'all ain't gone do nothing," said one of the other boys.

"What you say?" Tree said. "I don't know where y'all think y'all at, but y'all better go back to Montgomery with that."

The boy with the ball smiled. He said, "Everybody calm down." He held the basketball up. "Y'all want the ball?"

"Yeah," Vah said, holding out his hands for it.

"Go get it then," the boy said as he flung the ball as far he could into the park.

"Man, these goofies done lost they mind," Tutu said as he balled up his fist and started toward the boy that had thrown the ball.

Just in time Vah grabbed him and pointed with his head at the Chicago police car that had jumped the curb. The car cruised slowly down the park's path toward them. The boys from Montgomery High noticed the car too.

"Don't make a difference where we from, we 8 Deuce wherever we go," sneered another one of the boys.

"What boy?" Tree said. "We Gray Street Gang over here homie. The only reason y'all acting tough is 'cause them cops right there. "

The two officers that were assigned to the park and the school sat and watched the standoff from their vehicle.

"We don't rock with Gray Street goofies," said the boy that started the entire confrontation.

They had to hold Tutu and Tre back after that insult. Vah got close enough to the boy to read the name on his school ID hanging on a lanyard around his neck.

Vah said," Seems like y'all the ones acting tough because the cops right there, Shannon. You and the rest of these lames."

This time Shannon surged forward and had to be held by his friends. "Let me go Grant and Donnie, I'm finta beat this boy ass." His friends held onto him though.

Donnie said, "Chill boy, we ain't finta get locked up for they soft ass."

"Y'all might as well let Shannon go," Tutu said. "We already know he ain't finta do…"

The loudspeaker on the Chicago Police Department car squawked to life. "Alright boys break it up. Let's leave the park. Either go to school or go to jail, your choice. Clear the park now or sit in lockup until your mama come get you."

The mere mention of jail took the wind out of their sails. Mean mugging and glaring all the way, Tutu and his friends walked over to pick up their belongings.

"We'll see you girls around," Shannon called out as he and his friends walked away.

"You can count on that baby sis," Tutu promised.

"You can bet yo last dollar on that." To his friends he said, "Let's bounce y'all, I ain't finta be going to jail on my first day back because of some goofies."

Separately, both groups crossed the street to the school while keeping their eyes on one another.

CHAPTER 4

In Geography class, Tutu couldn't keep his eyes off of the clock on the wall. By his calculation there was like seven minutes to go before the bell rang and he could hardly wait. He was hungry hungry. He had smoked a blunt on the way to school with his friends and he hadn't eaten breakfast, so it felt like his stomach was touching his spine.

His book bag was already packed and he'd received the homework worksheet. At his school there weren't very many textbooks and many of them were outdated, so teachers relied on worksheets for classwork and homework. His geography teacher was a short, balding white man who probably should have retired some time ago. He usually smelled of beef jerky and pain ointment. Tutu really loved geography, hearing about all the different and exotic places in the world, but this teacher usually gave his lessons in a dry, monotone voice making the subject seem boring. It wouldn't have mattered today if his teacher was the most exciting man on Earth, the only thing on Tutu's mind was one of those cheeseburgers from the lunchroom with a mountain of French fries.

He fantasized about how he would put a handful

of French fries on top of his burger and use the bun to smash them down, before taking the biggest bite he could safely manage. It might have only been a cafeteria cheeseburger, affectionately known as a 'murder burger', but it was gone taste like a chopped steak with gyro meat and nacho cheese when he got ahold of it today. His stomach growled loudly protesting his self-imposed hunger strike and he had to look around to see if anyone heard it. The girl sitting next to him had heard it and she smiled at him. All he could do was smile back sheepishly.

The bell rang and Tutu was out of his seat and out of the classroom like he'd been shot out of a cannon. In the hallway, he zigzagged and dodged students as he ran through the hall and jumped down two flights of steps. On his journey two different security guards warned him to stop running. The first guard he ignored totally because he was a bit senile and slow, and he could never remember any of the students' names or faces. On the other hand, the second security guard, Officer Peters was as strict as they came and messing with him you could end up in in-school suspension, detention or out-of-school suspension so fast your head would spin. When Tutu spotted him, he slowed down until he was out of Officer Peters' line of sight, and then he took off again.

Downstairs on the first floor of the school, luckily the line for fifth period lunch had just begun to form and Tutu secured the eighth place in line. Each lunch period could easily contain a couple hundred students so he was thankful he had such a great spot in line. Already 10 more students were behind him and more were getting in line with every passing second. The cafeteria doors opened and the line began to move forward. He was licking his chops as he went through the doors. Soon he had a food tray in his hand, sliding it across the metal bars in front of the food. Today, as most days, there were several choices for lunch: mystery meat meatloaf with mashed potatoes with gray gravy, rubbery cheese pizza, and the cheeseburger he'd been waiting for all morning.

He passed the meatloaf and the pizza and as he stood in front of the lady handing out the cheeseburgers she looked at him questioningly.

"I want the cheeseburger and fries," he stated. "I been thinking about this all morning. You think I could get two of them Ms. Lunch Lady?"

"One sandwich per student per tray," the lunch server droned as she used her plastic gloved hand to put a cheeseburger on his tray. Tureon smiled his brightest smile as he turned on the charm.

"Can I at least have a few more fries, pretty please?"

The lunch lady looked at him for a second like she didn't know whether to snap on him or smile at him. Instead she did neither, she just grabbed a very large handful of French fries and put them on his tray.

"Next," she said in a bored tone.

Knowing not to press his luck with the lunch ladies, he moved on, sliding his tray to the milk and snack station. There, he collected his chocolate milk and a fruit cup. He walked to the cashier and showed her the free lunch punch on his school I.D., and she waved him past. In the seating part of the lunchroom he headed for the side of the large room where he usually shared a table with his friends and any girls they could convince to sit with them. As he got closer he could see the entire section where their table was located had been roped off and repairmen were working on the ceiling there.

"Damn," Tureon muttered as he detoured. He stuffed a few fries into his mouth as he started looking for an empty table; he found one and took a seat. He crammed fries into his mouth as he took the top bun off his burger and piled it high with French fries, using the bun to smash them down. He took a gigantic bite of his French fry cheeseburger as he watched more and more students filter into the lunchroom. As they filled up the tables, the noise level went up substantially in the room. There was loud laughter, rapping, beating on tables, students roasting one another, and even some older kids engaged in a hearty game of Spades.

A group of girls that must have been used to sitting at the table Tutu now occupied, stopped beside it and threw him major shade as they rolled their eyes and looked him up and down like they wanted to confront him.

One especially brave girl in the group said, "Aye boy, this our table."

With his mouth full of food, Tutu said, "I ain't see yo name on it nowhere. I should probably move hunh?"

"Yeah," she said smartly with her hand on her hip. Tutu laughed. "Girl, stay in school because you really stupid. Now push on."

The girl started to get worked up, but her friends steered her away. One of them said, "C'mon girl, that Negro is too petty for TV. He a lame anyway that's why he sitting by hisself. Let's bounce before somebody see us associating with this loser."

Tutu didn't verbally respond, he simply made an

obscene gesture and kept eating. As he ate, he kept his eyes peeled for his gang members, Tree and Air. They both had the same lunch period as him and they usually met up and walked to the cafeteria together, but today he was just too hungry to wait. He'd seen Tree earlier by the gym, but he hadn't seen Air today, so he didn't even know if he was in school. He shook his chocolate milk before he opened the carton and drained it. As he sat the empty container on his tray, he wished he had two dollars to get a Gatorade from the vending machine, but he didn't have a dime. He was using his teeth to open his spork packet while eating the remainder of his fries when he noticed Shannon, Grant and Donnie, all 8 Deuces Hotheads, coming his way carrying food trays.

Of late things had gotten real tense between the two gang factions at school; they had nearly come to blows on several occasions. The only thing that held the 8 Deuces somewhat in check was that they knew it was way more Gray Street Gang members in the school than them. Now that Tutu was alone, he knew this had the potential to go bad for him because he'd been caught lacking.

I really don't need this right now, he thought as he spooned fruit cocktail in his mouth. Now where Tree slow ass at? He knew it was too late to dip so he remained where he was and continued to eat. As the 8 Deuce boys drew nearer, Grant spotted him first and nudged Shannon directing his attention to Tutu sitting alone.

Shannon quickly assessed the situation as he looked around for any of Tutu's boys to make sure this wasn't a setup. When he didn't see any of them, he turned back with a wicked smirk on his face. He indicated to his friends to follow him to a table nearby. The two boys already seated at the table quickly recognized their unwanted tablemates, grabbed their trays and bags and relocated.

Tutu wanted to leave too, but he didn't want to appear scared so he kept his seat. The 8 Deuces kept looking his way as they talked amongst themselves. Tutu pretended to ignore them until one of them threw a tater tot over in his direction. The tater tot missed by a mile, but the disrespect it implied was evident as the boys that threw it fell all over themselves laughing. Tutu stood up and picked up his tray and his book bag to get ready and leave, when an entire orange came flying. This time he had to duck. He put his tray back down.

"Throw something else at me and see what happen," Tutu threatened. "Throw one more thing at me, I dare you."

Both Donnie and Grant looked to Shannon for his response. Shannon stood up. "Who you think you talking to boy? Yo boys ain't here to save you today, so you better watch yo mouth."

"Who gone make me watch my mouth? You?" Tutu asked as he dropped his bag onto the floor. "Do it look like I'm worried? All you 8 Deuce goofies do is make threats and don't back them up."

Shannon came from around the table. To his friends, he said, "C'mon y'all, I'm tired of his big ass mouth. He always trying to act tough, let's beat his ass." Donnie and Grant joined Shannon in surrounding Tutu in a semicircle.

"Boy you better stop playing with us," Donnie said

menacingly. "I don't know who you think you..."

Without warning Tutu struck Donnie with a vicious right cross to the jaw. There was a crunching sound as Donnie dropped to the ground. He held his jaw as he rolled around on the floor and howled. Tutu tried to recover quickly from the first punch and throw another one, but he was off balance as he launched it, missing Shannon by a mile. Grant however didn't miss as he punched Tutu squarely in the mouth. Shannon pushed him at the same time causing Tutu to go down on one knee to avoid being knocked over. Shannon began swinging wildly and Tutu had no choice but to cover his head and face.

Some of Shannon's punches connected but there wasn't any impact from them. From behind his guards, Tutu saw Grant drawing back his foot to kick him and braced himself to try and absorb the impact. All of a sudden, Tree and the boy that had spoken to him on the bus stop his first day back, dove onto Shannon and Grant, tackling them to the ground and pommeling them. Tutu got his feet and was about to rejoin the fray when someone grabbed him behind in a tight bear hug.

"Let me go!" Tutu snapped. "Let me the hell go." He swiveled his head to see who had him. It was the school's police officer, Officer Peters. To Peters, he said, "Let me go. They tried to jump me."

"Shut up boy, I saw you throw the first punch," Peters said. "I saw the whole thing."

In record time, the school's entire security force seemed to descend on the lunchroom. They made their way over to the brawling teenagers and in short order they pulled everyone apart and had them sorted out. They gathered up the boys and their belongings and escorted them to the disciplinarian's office in a not so gentle manner.

In the office, the boys talked back and forth continuing to threaten one another while Donnie sat and cried holding his jaw. Officer Peters grew tired of their voices and yelled, "The next person that say anything is going to jail! Now say something else!"

The threat of jail quieted the boys down and they seemed content to glare at one another, until the dean of discipline walked into the office and took a seat on the corner of the desk there. Mr. Paul, was a slight, but intense man, also he was considered a snappy dresser, pulled out a stick of gum and put it in his mouth.

He kept his eye on the boys as he said, "Officer Peters give me the meat and potatoes."

Peters peered at the collection of the boys' school IDs in front of him on the desk.

"Tureon Young punched Donnie George here, obviously breaking his jaw. George's friends retaliated leading into Young's friends coming to his rescue."

Mr. Paul scooped up all of their IDs and placed them in a line on the desk. "Okay then, we'll do it like this. Since Mr. Tureon Young thinks he's in the UFC or something, we'll give him five days suspension. Everyone else involved gets three days."

Tutu balked at his sentence and was prepared to protest, but Mr. Paul shushed him. "I don't want to hear it Mr. Young. Next time keep your hands to yourself. If someone is bothering you go tell a teacher, tell somebody like Officer Peters, hell come tell me. Now because of your actions, Mr. George here needs medical attention. Does anybody else from the security team wish to add anything?"

"What we have here is the start of some street gang beef that's spilling over in the school," offered a member of the security team. "So I'm almost sure that this isn't the last we've seen of this."

"Now that puts a different light on things, kiddies," Mr. Paul announced. "Being that this is a gang free zone, if and when you come back to campus if there's another altercation with gang overtones, everyone involved will receive a mandatory ten day suspension. If you make it back from that and there's another incident, you will be excluded from school; automatic expulsion. If you trespass on the campus after that you'll be arrested and prosecuted. Everyone understand?"

When no one answered, Mr. Paul said, "That's not a rhetorical question, meaning it requires an answer. Does everyone understand?"

This time either the boys mumbled yes or nodded their heads.

Mr. Paul stood and scooped up the boys' IDs. "Alright Officer Peters, staff, good job. I'll go complete the paperwork and drop it at the attendance office."

He saluted the boys and left the disciplinarian's office. The boys on the other hand had to wait to be dismissed.

CHAPTER 5

Tutu was bored almost to tears. He had been in the house for two days since he was suspended, not because he was in trouble with Meeka, but because it had rained both days. He had considered his suspension a sort of vacation, because he felt like he deserved a few days off from school. If he would have been able to go outside it wouldn't have been so bad, but with the steady rain keeping him in the house boredom had set in.

Today it had stopped raining, though it was still cloudy and gray. Tutu was sitting on the couch watching an episode of First 48 and flicking to Sportscenter during the commercials at the moment. He picked up his cell phone and just as he was about to go on Facebook and make a post about loyalty, his text message alert sounded; it was from Vah.

Vah: wyo

Tutu: no thing @ the crib

Vah: finta slide blow this bag

Tutu: slide

Vah: omw we gotta get woods

Tutu: ok cool

While he was waiting for Vah, he logged onto his

Facebook, made his post and began to scroll through, liking other people's posts and commenting on them here and there. Vah was taking forever so Tutu went out on the porch to wait for him. He alternated between watching the street and watching rap music videos while he waited. Just when he was about to text Vah to find out his location, he saw Vah turn the corner onto his block. Vah was walking with someone he didn't recognize until they got closer. It was the boy from the bus stop that helped him in the fight with Shannon and his boys in the lunchroom.

Vah walked up on the porch and shook hands with Tutu. He had a cigarette hanging from the corner of his mouth.

"Tutu, waddup gang," Vah said by way of greeting.

"Ain't nothing."

"Yo, this is Pooh," Vah explained. "He gang gang, he helped y'all on that move in the lunchroom. He from Spring Street too where Coolout and Beal be at. Shorty a real one, on God."

Tutu nodded his head at Pooh and held out his middle finger. Pooh accepted it and they did the Gray Street Gang handshake. Vah and Pooh both took a seat on the porch and they began to break the weed and Backwoods down so they could roll up.

"That was some good looking on that help up at the school," Tutu said. "It was finta go bad anyway so I stuck Donnie ass. He was talking when he should have been fighting. When I whacked his ass I lost my balance because I tried to punch Shannon ass real quick but he moved out the way. When I slipped they tried to get down on me, but they wasn't on nothing. They scratched me up more than anything."

Pooh said, "Me and Tree reacted when we saw what was happening. I'ma keep it a hondo, you wasn't going. You messed Donnie up bad too, buddy jaw wired right now."

"Yeah?" Tutu breathed with his lungs full of smoke.

"Hell yeah." Vah answered. "He online talking greasy through the wires though."

Pooh said, "Yeah homie been going live woofin' hard. He said even though his jaw broke he can still smoke on Tyrese from Gray Street."

"Okay, okay we gone have to see about that," Tutu promised. "I guarantee you homie was acting all tough, but when I cracked his ass in his jaw, he was rolling around on the floor crying like a baby."

"Well now he be online fronting his move like he with whatever," Pooh said.

"Straight out his body," Vah agreed as he exhaled weed smoke.

"I'ma get Donnie, but who I really want is Shannon," Tutu said emotionally. He slammed his fist into the palm of his hand. "I hate that boy! He swear he so hard but he don't make a move without them send-offs that be with him. I can't wait to catch that boy in traffic, I'ma do him so dirty."

"On God," Pooh agreed.

As the weed began to take effect, they all fell silent and soon they were all texting and scrolling through social media on their respective cell phones. Every so often one of them would show the others a funny meme, or if someone was going hard on their page. Vah turned his music on and they were content to chill until Pooh said, "Hell nall. Check this out, here go yo boy 8 Deuce Donnie."

Pooh offered his phone to Tutu. Donnie was videotaping himself live on Instagram in all of his wire-mouthed glory. Tutu pushed the volume button on the side of the phone until it was at its max.

"...up here at the dollar store to buy me some Ensure because I can't eat no food. Yeah, them lames from Gray Street jumped me up at school. I was beating Tutu ass when one of them snaked me from the back with a lucky punch. That's alright though, because when I catch GSG Tutu I'm gone put my feet on him and that's on gang nem. So if they laughing, they better laugh now because they gone cry later and that's on my Granny." Donnie turned the camera on two girls as they walked past him in the store. He turned the camera back onto himself. "Uh-oh, THOT alert, look like we got some eaters on deck."

One of the girls stopped the other girl from walking. She turned to Donnie and to the girl she was with, she said, "Slow down friend, for some reason this goofy is confusing us with his mama. I don't know how that happened, cause ain't neither one of us old, and we both got all our hair and teeth. It's alright though because I got the feeling it'll never happen again."

"You better watch yo mouth," Donnie warned through the wires in his mouth.

"You obviously didn't," the girl retorted.

"Okay, keep talking. On Eight Deuce I'll slap both of y'all."

The other girl pulled her friend by the arm out of the aisle. "C'mon Tracy, ain't nobody got time for these broke boys, they be big mad. Them the ones be trying to put they hands on you and mess up yo face. Let's go."

"You birds better get lost, before it be a problem up in here," Donnie threatened as he used his phone's camera to follow the girls' exit. His camera captured the opposite side of the street through the store's windows in his next shot. "Y'all got me messed up."

On Tureon's porch, Vah was excited when he said, "Man, this goofy at the Family Dollar right there on the Nine."

"You sure, Vah?" Tutu asked. "Please tell me you sure. The one right there by the Subway and the liquor store cross the street?"

"Yup," Vah reaffirmed. "The taco spot right there on the corner and the auto part store sign is down the block from there next to the gas station. What y'all wanna do?"

"Are you kidding?" Tutu asked sarcastically as he got up. He was still heated about Donnie's comments about his dead brother. He went inside the apartment, and pulled on a pair of shoes and got his door keys. He left out and locked the door behind himself. Outside on the porch to Vah and Pooh, he said, "C'mon. It's only a few blocks away and if we hurry up, we prolly can catch his sneakdissin ass."

The three boys scampered down the stairs and took off at a dead run in the direction of the Nine. They slowed down to a jog after a block and a half, but they kept going. When they reached the Nine, they just had to make it two streets over to get to the Family Dollar store. They slowed down to catch their breath as they walked the rest of the way to the store. Vah said, "Pooh, check yo phone and see if his lame ass still on there cappin." Pooh checked his Instagram. "Yeah he still in the store. He finta leave out now, he in line."

"C'mon y'all," Tutu ordered. "Soon as this vic come out the door we finta flood his ass." The trio crossed the street and posted up outside the entrance to the store. They only had to wait a short time before Donnie came walking out the store's automatic door. He was still holding up his phone, recording as he walked and carried his bag of purchases. As soon as he came out the second door, Pooh snatched his phone.

"Aye, gimme my phone boy!" Donnie said a split second before he noticed Vah.

Without a word, Donnie threw his bag at Vah as he turned to run, but instead he ran smack dab into Tutu, who scooped him by the legs and slammed him to the ground. Using their hands and feet, Tutu and Vah made quick work of Donnie, while Pooh recorded the entire beating with Donnie's phone. It didn't take too long with the ferocity of the beating they were issuing out for them to grow winded. Donnie wasn't moving much as their punches lost some of their sting and their kicks became more infrequent. As Tutu stood up to catch his breath, he pointed at the camera.

"Pooh make sure you get all this," Tutu said as he walked over and picked up two bottles of Donnie's Ensure. They had rolled from the bag when Donnie threw it. He shook the bottles up as he returned to stand over Donnie.

Into the camera he said, "This boy shole had a lot to say a minute ago, but he gone learn to watch his mouth today." Tutu dumped the contents of one bottle, then the next on Donnie's head and face. "I already broke his jaw, but it seem like that wasn't enough so he gone learn today."

Pooh and Vah laughed as Donnie gasped and wriggled

around in the nutritional drink Tutu had poured on him. Vah got in front of the camera and said, "Just so you 8 Deuces know, stay off the Nine woofin before you get beat up. Matter fact y'all lucky we only kicked his ass."

The automatic door of the store swung open and the store manager stood in the doorway. "Aye shorties, y'all leave him alone, he done had enough. Y'all gone on and let him be now."

The boys started to run off laughing when suddenly Vah made a U-turn. He ran back to the prone Donnie, rolled him over onto his back and unbuckled his designer belt. He tugged the belt loose from the groaning boy's pants belt loops. Vah rolled Donnie back onto his stomach and used his belt to beat his butt with it until Donnie balled up in a fetal position to protect himself from the blows. Pooh could barely keep the camera steady as he and Tutu fell all over themselves laughing at Donnie's plight.

"C'mon gang," Tutu called to Vah. To the camera he said, "That's what we mean when we say we gone whup one of y'all ass. Gray Street!"

Vah ran and caught up to them as they ran off laughing. Tutu saw that he wasn't carrying the belt.

"What you do with Donnie's belt?" he asked.

"I left it, it was fake anyway. Gas station ass belt. Loose square man ass belt. 20 dollars left on my Link card ass belt."

They all laughed as Pooh handed Tutu Donnie's phone. "Man, you need this more than us, Tutu. Now you can throw that bogus Android gov-o phone away." Laughing Pooh ran away.

"Did he just call the droid a gov-o phone?" Tutu

asked.

"Yup," Vah said, as he took off running too. "He wasn't lying."

"Man, y'all bogus," Tutu said as he ran after his friends.

CHAPTER 6

Tutu got out of his bed and put his feet in his Nike slides. He went to the bathroom to empty his bladder. It was now Saturday afternoon, he'd slept completely through the morning. He had gotten in late last night and he was as high as a kite. Meeka had never really been too strict with his curfew, and it was rarely mentioned these days.

As he stood over the toilet doing his business, he noticed how strong his urine was smelling and how dark it was, and made a mental note to drink more water and juice. Along with his friends and gang members, he had been celebrating his 16th birthday for over a week now. He had never seen or smoked so much weed in his life. It seemed like Geno had an endless supply of the stuff.

Right now all he wanted was something to eat. He had eaten three chicken wings from out of the pan of 50 wings they had from Sharks last night, but the chicken disappeared so fast he didn't get a chance to get any more. At this moment it felt like he hadn't eaten in a year.

Tutu flushed the toilet and made a beeline from the bathroom to the kitchen to find something to munch on. There were several boxes of cereal on top of the fridge, but it was cereal he wasn't interested in like Raisin Bran and Frosted Flakes. Also, since his mother had been buying 2% milk of late, he rarely had a taste for cereal. He checked the cabinets; no Pop-Tarts or granola bars, just Vienna sausages, sardines and Ramen noodles.

"Damn!" he said aloud. He closed the cabinets and went over and opened the fridge. In the refrigerator there were eggs, bottles of water, an empty Kool-Aid pitcher, some mystery leftovers, a couple of his mother's turkey hotdogs and some apples that had seen better days. As he viewed the contents of the refrigerator, he said, "Man, Meeka need to go shopping."

He looked over on the table to see if there was some bread. He figured he would settle out of court for a couple of jelly sandwiches, but there were only the two end slices left in the knotted bread bag on the table. He made a face because he'd sworn long ago to never eat the bootie slices of bread for any reason. He closed the refrigerator and left the kitchen to look for his mother.

He knocked on Meeka's bedroom door and when she didn't answer, he opened it. Her bed was made and she was nowhere in sight. He went to check the living room; she wasn't there either. He went back to his room and got his phone to give her a call and find out her location.

She picked up her end on the second ring. "What you want, Tutu?"

"Mama, where you at? I hope you at the grocery store, cause ain't nothing in here to eat."

"That's what you called me for, boy? I'm at work."

He looked at the wall like there was a calendar there.

"I know I ain't tweaking. Today is Saturday, yo day off."

"I went in for some overtime," Meeka admitted. "I didn't feel like sitting around all day doing nothing when I coulda been getting to the bag. I might work tomorrow too."

"Maaaaa, when you gone go shopping?" he whined.

"Its food in there boy. You better make you some noodles or something. Its cereal and milk in there too."

Tutu balled up his face at the mere mention of either of those foods. "I don't want none of that, Ma. I'm noodled out and I ain't drinking that watery milk. I want some restaurant food."

"Well, I don't know what to tell you," Meeka said. "I'm at work boy."

"Ma, please. Please I'm hungry."

Meeka sighed. "Shuddup. Look boy, go in my room, it's a 20 dollar bill on the tote by my bed. Get it and get you $10 and bring back my change. Nall, better yet, catch the square man and get me a pack of cigarettes." Happily, he skipped out of his bedroom and back into his mother's room. He easily found the money and went back to his room to get dressed. The whole time his mother had been talking on the phone, but he hadn't heard much after she said he could have some money.

Back in his room, into the phone, he said, "Thanks, Ma. I'm finta go get some food right now Meeka. I love you."

"Don't forget my squares," Meeka said, but a click on the line let her know he'd already hung up. She also knew better than to try and call him back, he would just ignore her call, so she sent him a text message.

Meeka: Don't 4get my squares boy

Tutu: I got u OG

Meeka returned her cell phone to her apron pocket and took her toilet brush and disinfectant and headed for the bathroom of the room she was cleaning.

At home in his room, Tutu pulled on a black pair of Adidas jogging pants with white stripes down the leg. He slipped his feet into the Concorde Mikes, he'd gotten last week for his birthday, and put on his black Polo bubble jacket. He went to get his gun from under the pillow, but he remembered he'd let Pooh borrow it to go to the Westside to see some girl.

"Gotta get my gun back from Pooh, Asap Rocky," he said aloud. "I ain't finta be out here naked just 'cause he wanna go see some random chick."

The fact that he didn't have his weapon didn't deter him one bit from going to the restaurant. He let himself out of the apartment and locked the door. Outside he cut across the street and jogged through a couple of vacant lots until he was on the next street. He was headed to the Nine where he would find the cigarette man and the restaurant he wanted to get his food from there.

At the corner store on the next block he looked around until he saw the cigarette man Meeka bought her squares from. He was across the street in the parking lot of the currency exchange. He trotted across the street and made the purchase for his mother. Once he received his change, he was on his way to get his food. The restaurant he planned on ordering from was a mere two streets east of there.

As he walked, his mind jumped around to a lot of different things to eat: jerk or fried chicken, a gyro with mild sauce, a buffalo chicken Philly cheesesteak or some tacos. All of these were some of his favorite foods, but they just wouldn't do right now. He had a taste for a gym shoe sandwich made his way. A gym shoe was a sub sandwich made with gyro meat, corned beef and roast beef with mayo, lettuce, tomato and cheese. In his version, he substituted the roast beef with Italian beef meat, gyro sauce for mayo, and had them heat the sandwich. Just thinking about it made him want to pick up his pace.

In the neighborhood sandwich shop, he ordered his gym shoe sub, and clutching his food ticket and receipt, he took a seat in a rickety booth with an orange table. The booth where he was seated had definitely seen better days. To take his mind off of his wait for his food, he decided to check his social media sites. He was grinning at an exceptionally gross comedian on Instagram when the door to the restaurant swung inward. Two girls, maybe a year or two older than him, walked into the restaurant.

Though they walked past him like he didn't exist, Tutu checked them out from head to toe, especially the taller of the two girls. He could swear he knew her from somewhere. She was slim, but hippy, wearing some grey leggings that he instantly approved of as she walked past.

At the restaurant's bulletproof glass in front of the cashier, the girls asked for their call-in order. The food they ordered was ready so they paid for it, checked their bags and turned to leave. As they were leaving, for the first time the girls noticed Tutu; he did know the taller one. They had went to the same grade school, though she was in a higher grade. The shorter of the two was a chubby, light-skinned, big nosed girl wearing long braids that had seen better days with a dark scowl on her face. The tall girl's pretty brown face immediately brightened as she looked at him.

"Hey Tutu," said the tall girl pleasantly.

"Hey Carmisha," Tutu said. "I ain't seen yo pretty self in a while. How you been?"

"I been good. I was staying outta town for a minute, but we just moved back. Everybody just call me Misha now. What you been on?"

"I ain't been on anything. What's up though? Who is yo friend?"

The scowl on the chubby girl's face grew even darker, like a storm cloud over a picnic. Misha pulled on her friend's arm.

"You gotta excuse my friend, Mimi. She dealing with some family issues right now."

"Oh, I'm sorry to hear that baby girl," Tutu said. "Let me know if there's anything I can do."

"I don't want nobody in my family business," Mimi snapped as she rolled her neck and eyes. "You need to mind yo business, that's how people get hurt."

Tutu was taken aback. "Damn, lil baby, why you so pressed? You is doing way too much. But that's on me, I'm gone make sure I stay up out yo business and yo face. My bad. Maybe you just hungry, I'll fall back and let y'all go eat y'all food maybe you'll feel better."

Mimi rolled her eyes again as she said, "Misha, let's go before my food get cold."

"Alright Tutu," Misha said, as she turned to follow Mimi from the restaurant.

"I'ma look you up on the Gram or the Book and hit you up, see what you on Misha," Tutu called out as he returned his attention to his cell phone.

"Yeah, do that," Misha said with another bright smile before leaving out the restaurant.

Outside the sub shop, on the sidewalk, Mimi was almost stomping as she strode away from the restaurant. Misha's legs were long so she easily kept pace with her shorter friend.

"Mimi, slow down girl," Misha said. "Girl, I'm about to have to run to keep up with you."

"Well you better bring yo butt on before I leave you," Mimi seethed. "You got the nerve to be in there key-key-keying with that opp and you know what they did to my cousin Donnie. That's crazy! He actually in there on Donnie's phone. We gone see bout this."

Misha rolled her eyes to the sky. "Now how would I know that? What you finta do Mimi?"

"Uhhh, behave loyally, something you seem to know nothing about," Mimi said as she pulled her cell phone from her back pocket. Her phone was dead so she put it back in her pocket and held out her hand. "Gimme yo phone."

Reluctantly Misha handed over her cell phone. "Look girl, I don't want my name in nobody mess," she warned. "I ain't playing neither. I got friends from Gray Street and 8 Deuce so I don't take sides. It's all stupid to me and I wish they would grow up."

Mimi accepted the phone, handed Misha her food bag and dialed a number from memory as she walked a bit away from Misha. Soon Mimi was yelling into the phone and gesturing with her hands as she explained the situation with tears in her eyes. Misha took that time to sit on the curb while she waited and pulled her chicken wing dinner from her bag. She had eaten two of the wings from her six wing dinner by the time Mimi ended her call. Mimi walked back to Misha and stood over her. She extended her phone down to her, but Mimi was so busy eating she didn't see it.

"Here girl, get yo phone," Misha said snippily. "We need to move around. My people said to get from up here on the Nine. Come on with yo greedy self."

Misha took her time putting her chicken dinner back in the bag. She got her phone from Mimi and handed her food back to her as she stood up. She wiped her butt off and stepped up on the curb.

"C'mon girl, let's get from around here, before you be done got us killed," Misha said while giving Mimi a weird look. "I got to stop messing with you, you act like one of these dudes."

In the restaurant, Tutu was playing a game on his phone as he waited for his food. One of the restaurant workers behind the bulletproof glass came to the window and looked at him as he held up a plastic bag of food. The worker said, "What you want on fries? What kind of pop?"

Tutu sprung from the booth and went to the window. He was so happy his food was ready, he drummed a beat on the counter.

"Mild sauce and lemon pepper on my fries and a grape Crush."

The employee put his pop in the bag and dressed his fries with several squirts of mild sauce and a couple of shakes of the lemon pepper shaker. He added a drinking straw and napkins to the bag before he put it in the Plexiglas carousel, and spun it around so he could get his food.

Tutu left the sub shop and walked down the street swinging his bag as he ate French fries out of it. The fries were so hot and delicious he was humming as he walked along eating them. He was a street over and a block away from home when he passed an abandoned house with overrun bushes. As he got closer to the house, he pulled out his phone to turn on some music. He was searching for a song in his phone when someone stepped out of the bushes wearing a black hoodie and a mask. Tutu looked up at the figure that suddenly appeared in front of him.

"Aye boy, you gone learn to keep yo hands to yo'self," the masked man said as he raised his gun and pointed it at Tutu.

Before he could say or do anything, the gunman opened fire. Tutu didn't hear the shots until several seconds later, though he felt the bullets ripping into his flesh. He didn't know how many times he'd been hit, but knew it was a lot, yet the gunman was still shooting. The last thing he could remember was staggering backwards from the impact of the shots before the bullets knocked him over. As he fell, his food bag hit the dirt as he dropped it and the contents spilled out. His sandwich rolled out of the wrapper and fell apart. The few fries he had left fell into the dirt too.

As he lay in the dirt looking at his food, he waited for the assassin to come stand over him and finish the job; though he didn't. Instead the shooter ran away, leaving him lying there as his blood mingled with the French fries on the ground.

CHAPTER 7

"...he's still breathing," Tutu heard someone say as his eyes popped open. "Get back! Get back! Give him some air."

The mention of the word air made him realize that he needed to breathe, so he drew the longest, harshest, most painful breath he'd ever drawn in his life. The breath he took felt like he was swallowing rusty razor blades as he inhaled. The air tasted and felt like it was dirty and corroded as he pulled it into his lungs.

He wanted to sit up and try to clear his airway, but as he shifted just a millimeter, the pain of his bullet wounds dropped a nuclear bomb of nerve-shredding pain on his nervous system.

"Aaaaaaaaahhhhhhhhhh!" he moaned long and loudly as he slipped back down and closed his eyes.

Someone knelt next to him and said, "Take it easy little buddy. Stay with us. Help is on the way. Don't give up now." The stranger snapped his fingers in Tutu's ear several times to get his attention and try and bring him out of his stupor. "You can't go to sleep right now little brother. No time to rest now."

To Tutu each finger snap sounded like a gunshot, but they did succeed in making him a tiny bit more alert. Another person took his hand into theirs, and he could tell from the size and softness of the hand, it was a woman.

In a soft, almost melodic voice, she begged him, "Please breathe young brother. I know it may be hard but you have to try. Please don't give up."

There was so much emotion and care in her voice, Tutu decided to try again, but when he did, the pain he experienced from taking a few smaller, ragged breaths made him pass out again.

The lady's shoulders shook as she began to weep, but she never let go of his hand. The crowd around them had grown considerably and more people were joining it every second, trying to get a glimpse of the shooting victim. Several people were openly recording what looked like his last breaths.

A group of boys came running up the street, three of them had their guns drawn as they ran to the scene. At the same time, a car screeched to a halt in the street and Geno, Danno and Price bailed out of it. Impolitely they pushed their way through the crowd. Tree, Pooh and Con joined them in the middle of the crowd. The older guy that had snapped his fingers in Tutu's ear spotted the guns the boys were holding and spoke up. "Y'all not about to do anything else to this boy. Haven't y'all done enough?"

Geno looked at the older guy like he wanted to shoot him in the chest. In fact, he was raising his gun when Price stepped in between them and pushed Geno's arm down.

"Look old head, this our homie right here, he gang," Price explained. "We ain't do this. Best thing you can do right now is move back. We got our guy."

While Price was checking the man for trying to protect Tutu, Danno, Con and Geno stooped down next to him to see if he was dead. They were slightly relieved when they saw his chest was still fluttering up and down as he took labored breaths. It was a good sign because at least he was still breathing.

"Lil bro, lil bro," Danno said, trying to get his attention. "Tutu, who did this to you? Can you hear me? Who shot you, Tutu?"

At the sound of Danno's voice, Tutu tried to open his eyes, but he couldn't manage it. He tried to talk, but he wasn't able to gather enough breath to do so. He seemed to be taking in too much wind and ended up only making a gurgling noise which Danno leaned in to hear, but couldn't make sense of. Danno stood to his feet with tears in his eyes. He had seen enough death in his young life to know his young friend was a goner. He looked at his friends as his tears began falling and shook his head.

What he say, what he say?" Con asked, more to himself than anyone else.

Danno just kept shaking his head sadly. "He ain't say nothing, he finta…"

"Hush now y'all," the lady holding his hand said. "Be quiet with that, he ain't gone nowhere. We need positive energy surrounding him right now. His soul is fighting for his life and he needs positive vibes right now. If you want to do something, pray for him. Ask the Universe or whatever you believe in to hold him here."

In spite of her words, Con broke into tears at the plight of his friend, while Tree just stood there with a befuddled look on his face. "I gotta call his OG," Con announced miserably, "I gotta call Meeka."

"Here come the ambulance!" someone yelled.

The ambulance was a block south of the scene and had slowed down like they were looking for an address. Some of the people in the crowd stepped into the street and hooped and hollered to get the ambulance's attention. The EMTs must have spotted the people flagging them down because they sped up and came forward to where the crowd was surrounding Tutu. As the paramedics got out of the ambulance, two police cars flew up the block and skidded to a halt. The armed GSG members faded through the crowd and made their escape through the first available gangway.

The paramedics, a stocky, football player looking white guy, and a young, pretty Black woman wearing her silky, black hair in a ponytail, rushed over to Tutu as the crowd parted out of their way. The lady holding his hand let it go and moved out of their way too, though she didn't go far.

After quickly assessing the situation, the male EMT ran back to the ambulance to get the gurney. He rolled it over to Tutu and the two of them heaved him onto it rougher than the crowd would have liked to see. They started to surge forward thinking he was being mishandled, but by now the policemen had exited their vehicles and held the crowd at bay.

"Back it up!" the different policemen ordered. "Everybody back up now! Let them do their job! Back up now! Don't make us call for a wagon! If you don't want to go to jail get back! Everyone step back!"

One of the officers retrieved a roll of crime scene tape from their vehicle and started to cordon off the immediate area. The paramedics had secured Tutu on the gurney and repacked their equipment bags. They pushed the gurney to the rear of the ambulance as one officer held up the yellow tape so they could go under it. They bumped the gurney up into the rear of the ambulance, climbed in with him and closed the doors behind them. Some of the people in the crowd stood on their tiptoes to look through the ambulance's door windows to see what they were doing to him.

The EMTs swiftly hooked him up to the monitors, and did their best to stabilize him for transport to the new trauma center at the University of Chicago. The male paramedic climbed into the driver's seat of the vehicle and started it up. At the rear of the ambulance, the lady that had been holding Tutu's hand placed both of her palms on the ambulance doors and whispered a prayer to the Ancestors and the Universe on his behalf. When she was finished she walked away hugging herself, with a knowing smile on her pretty, brown face.

The ambulance pulled away from the scene. It moved slowly at first, but quickly picked up speed as the driver turned on the lights and sirens. In the rear of the ambulance, the EMT did her best to monitor Tutu's extremely weak vital signs. She called ahead to the emergency room trauma center to make them aware of the incoming patient's condition. For the majority of the ride, there wasn't much of a change to Tureon's condition. Besides the monitors, the only indication he was still alive was the taxing breaths he would take every so often. His blood pressure was dangerously low so she called the ER and told them.

To her partner, she said, "Hey Piedmont, you would wanna step on it before we lose this guy."

"Alright, Sparrow," Piedmont said with a nod. He blew several loud blasts of the horn as he accelerated through a busy intersection.

They were a little over a mile from the hospital when his blood pressure bottomed out and his vital signs crashed. The monitors went crazy as his heart stopped beating.

"Piedmont, step on it, we're losing this guy!" Sparrow yelled as she began CPR. It took all of her skill and training, but she managed to get his heart restarted and his heart rate registered on the monitor again. She breathed a small sigh of relief as she pulled off the blood covered rubber gloves on her hands and donned a fresh pair.

Within minutes the ambulance was nosing its way into one of the ambulance bays at the hospital emergency room. The trauma center staff were on standby, waiting with a bed to transfer the patient from the ambulance gurney. Piedmont reversed the rig until one of the nurses slapped the side of the vehicle twice.

From the moment the back doors of the ambulance opened, the emergency room staff worked like a well-trained unit as they transferred Tutu to their bed, and rushed him through the automatic doors to emergency surgery.

In the emergency operating room, they were prepping him for surgery when he woke again. At first, lying on the table all he could see was the white lights overhead and he panicked, struggling weakly to sit up which only caused him more pain. Two of the nurses that were cleaning him off in preparation for the operation did their best to calm him down. His loss of blood, coupled with the pain made him slip back into unconsciousness. The last thing he saw was a group of doctors and nurses to the left of him getting dressed for surgery. As they grew blurry, it crossed his mind that they were either angels or demons, and depending on whether Tyrese was in heaven or hell, they were there to take him to his brother.

···

The surgeon elbowed the large metal button on the wall that triggered the automated doors. As the doors swung open, he rolled his head around to get the kinks out of his neck left there by a nine-hour surgery. The booties he wore over his Adidas running shoes made a swishing sound as he walked. He untied his mask from behind his neck and freed it from his face. He balled it up and threw it into the first wastebasket he walked past.

He had been off of work for over two hours now, and after such a long procedure, all he wanted was a thick porterhouse steak with a garden salad, a good cigar and some single malt whiskey. All of that would have to wait though until he talked to the patient's family waiting in the E.R. operating waiting room.

He opened the door to the waiting room area; it seemed there were people sitting or lying down on every available surface in the room. Some of them were even sleeping on the floor. There was a heated conversation going on between several parties, and everyone else seemed to be on their cell phones.

"Excuse me, I'm Dr. Renolt," the surgeon said, which caused them to pay attention to him for the first time since he'd stepped into the room. "I'm looking for the parents of Tureon Young."

The twins, Shameeka and Shaneeka stood up and came forward. "This is his mother," Neeka announced indicating Shameeka. "And I'm his favorite auntie."

"Well," the doctor said. "I've got news about Tureon, would you like to step into the hallway or…"

"Say what you gotta say man," Meeka said nervously. "We all his family in one way or another."

Dr. Renolt shrugged. "Okay, we lost Tureon on the table several times," he started.

"Ooooooohhhhh noooo, my baby," wailed Meeka. "They done killed my baby!"

"No, no, no ma'am," the surgeon said, holding his hands up. "I'm so so sorry for the mix up. Tureon is alive. He did die more than once on the table, but we were able to bring him back. As we speak he's in post op waiting to be transferred to his room in the intensive care unit. It's still touch and go for right now, with the first 24 hours being the hardest, but we have an excellent staff here so if there are any complications they'll be right on top of things."

"Doctor, how many times was he shot?" Neeka asked. "What type of damage is there? Will he still be able to walk?"

"Near as we can tell he's got seven bullet wounds. So far we aren't seeing any trauma to the spine and fortunately we were able to save his lung."

Tutu's aunt on his father's side of the family asked, "So what can we do doctor? What does he need?"

The surgeon answered, "Right now he needs you all to keep your fingers crossed. He's stable right now, but like I said, the first 24 hours are the most critical. After that, infection is our worst enemy. He'll be in a drug-induced coma for the next few days, so outside of his immediate family, no one is allowed in ICU. I really have to applaud my staff because they did everything in their power to get him to where we weren't having a totally different conversation right now. Keep some positive thoughts and prayers because he has a long way to go, but for now it seems the worst is over. Now if you'll excuse me, I'm going to get some rest."

Before the doctor could exit, Tutu's loved ones surged forward to thank him and shake his hand. Neeka noticed the uncomfortable look on the surgeon's face from such an emotional outpouring so she rescued him. "Let him gone on now," Neeka said. "Let him go, he tired now. He got more lives to save, let him gone get his rest. Thank you, Dr."

Neeka could tell he was grateful to her for calling for his release as he beat a hasty retreat. In the hallway, he made a beeline for a hand sanitizer dispenser on the wall before he went to go change to leave the hospital.

In the emergency operation waiting area, Tutu's friends and family were now smiling and laughing because he'd made it. Meeka went over to the couch where she'd been sitting with Neeka and got her purse. She turned to her twin sister.

"C'mon chick, we going outside to have a smoke and a drank."

Neeka didn't argue as she went to get her purse. "Sounds like a plan to me," she said.

CHAPTER 8

Tutu was lying on his hospital bed watching the Maury show on television. He was wearing two hospital gowns, one turned to the front and the other turned to the back and a pair of tan hospital footies to complete his outfit.

Since he'd moved out of ICU ten days ago, he'd been in a double room, but so far the other bed in his room had been empty the last few days. The room was empty when he first came so he had a choice of bed, and had chosen the bed nearest the large window. His bedroom window at home looked out at a brick wall three feet away, so he really enjoyed the view of the city the window gave him. At night there wasn't really much of anything on the television so often he would sit in the easy chair by the window, and look out at the city as he wrote rap lyrics in his cell phone.

His pain was nowhere near the level it was when he first transferred to this floor. Before he left the intensive care unit they weaned him off the Fentanyl, a powerful painkiller because with continued use of it, there was a strong chance of becoming addicted to it. They put him on some lesser meds and had the nurses teach him to manage the pain.

The holes in his flesh had mostly closed, and luckily he hadn't had any setbacks due to infection. He was walking without much of a problem, though he was stiff. Daily the staff took him for walks around the floor, two or three times a day, and the only problem he seemed to have was because of a collapsed lung; he would be out of breath after short distances and have to rest. He could tell that he was getting stronger every day though.

As he was waiting to find out whether the guy on the Maury show was the father or not, a hospital food service worker knocked on his half open room with his lunch tray.

"Young?" she asked as she entered the room.

"Yup," he answered.

She walked over and placed his tray and a menu on his tray table. "They said fill out the breakfast and lunch portion of the menu for tomorrow, but don't worry about dinner."

"Okay," Tutu agreed as he sat up in his bed and swung his legs off the side. His did this without too much discomfort. He wasn't surprised about not filling out the dinner menu, because the charge nurse had already told him more than likely he would be discharged tomorrow afternoon. The food service worker left as he pulled the bedside tray table that held his lunch tray closer. It had become a habit of his to eat his meals looking out the window. He took the heavy brown lid off the plate. No surprises there, a cheeseburger and salad. Also on the tray was a cup of peaches, a chocolate pudding cup, tea and juice.

When he first transferred to this unit, he was only able to drink liquids and take a few bites of solid food, but after a couple of days of that, his appetite returned with a vengeance. It took some getting used to, but soon he was eating the hospital food like it had been prepared by a gourmet chef. The cheeseburger he was eating now reminded him slightly of the cafeteria cheeseburgers at his school. He couldn't wait until the day he could eat another lunchroom burger covered in French fries.

He was eating his cup of peaches when it really hit him--he was getting out of here tomorrow. After almost a month. It would be an understatement to say he was having mixed feelings about his imminent release. His time here had given him a lot of time to think and write lyrics about everything: his brother's death, his near death, and the constant fighting and shooting in his neighborhood. He actually felt a bit lost as he wondered how many other 16 year old boys had to deal with so much stress.

Though he wanted to, and he thought some of them must have felt the same way, he couldn't talk to his friends about these kinds of thoughts. They would say he was acting soft because he'd just been shot. He could almost hear Danno's voice say, "They kilt yo brother and tried to kill you, Tutu, you can't never let that ride."

Since his brother's death, because of Danno and Geno, he had gotten a chance to be around some of the OG's, the Original Gangsters, from Gray Street, and they weren't anything like he thought they would be. He could tell many of them loved the streets and the gang, but in his mind, they were too old to act the way they did. Many of the founding members of the Gray Street Gang had died or been locked up long ago.

When it came to the ongoing war with the 8 Deuces, it shocked him to find out that many of them couldn't tell you why, when, or where it all started with any real certainty. That didn't stop them from being any less committed to the cause though.

Tutu turned up the cup and drank the syrup left from his peaches. He covered the tray and pushed the tray table out of the way so he could get up and walk to the window. He looked out at the life teeming around the University hospital. People were walking their dogs, riding bikes, holding hands as they pushed babies in strollers, jogging, and just seemed to be enjoying themselves and their lives. He knew because of their neighborhood, the lives they lived were so far from the lives, people like him lived in places like Gray Street. The kind of life that left his older brother dead, and him at the ripe old age of 16 fighting for his life in a trauma center. When he was writing his raps, it felt like he was writing to inform the people that didn't know what people like him were going through every day.

He was reminded of when he was much younger, he would be watching television and Tyrese would come into whatever room he was in and take the television remote control and change the channel. He would run to their mother to whine about how it wasn't fair, but her response was always, "Life ain't fair, get used to it." That didn't mean much to a child, but he understood what she meant by it a whole lot better now. Life was unfair, get over it.

Someone knocking on his room door startled him out of his thoughts. He turned to see it was one of the nurse's assistants.

"Hi Tureon," she said cheerfully, "Transportation is on their way to get you for your therapy, so get dressed."

"Okay," he said.

To get dressed, he simply pulled on a pair of jogging pants under his gowns. As he did, another small pinch of sadness hit him. He knew this was going to be his last session with the therapist. His physical therapist was a cheery, Latino woman named Karla, that had basically taught him to breathe again without straining so much. She was hard on her patients, but she encouraged them every step of the way. As he did the exercises she planned for him, he felt his strength returning, though he knew it would be quite a while before he was anywhere near 100 percent.

During his stay in the hospital, his mother Meeka would come every day at first, and then as he got better, she scaled it back to every other day. She was usually drunk or tired from work when she arrived, so she often spent the better part of her visits sleeping in the easy chair next to his bed. Either that or talking on her cell phone while going back and forth outside to smoke cigarettes. His auntie Neeka came almost every day. Her personality was always warmer than his mother's and she was much easier to talk to than Meeka.

His friends came a few times in the beginning, but their attendance dried up quickly. Vah told him they were heavily into it with 8 Deuces, so everybody had to be on point at all times; no lacking while it's cracking. There were casualties on both sides of the feud, but so far no one had died, except the girl named Mimi, that he met in the restaurant the day he got shot. She was riding in the car with some of the opps, when somebody from Gray Street shot their car up on the expressway. She died from her wounds at the scene. Misha told him about it when she came to visit him though she didn't seem as sad as he thought she would be. In fact, Misha visited him quite a few times during his stay. He had come to look forward to her visits. She was so funny, sometimes she would have his bullet wounds aching from laughing at her. He still texted and talked to several other girls, but he found himself thinking about Misha more than any of them.

The only other recent fatality was a nine year old boy. He was walking with his mother on the Nine when a car full of 8 Deuce members tried to kill a GSG member named Pogo. Pogo was leaving the Chinese food restaurant on the Nine, near Pierce Street when some 8 Deuces opened fire from a passing car. They missed Pogo completely, besides hitting his container of shrimp fried rice, and succeeded in grazing the young mother and shooting her nine year old. The boy died instantly from his gunshot wounds.

The little boy's death was tragic, but Tutu knew that's how it goes in the streets. For a few days everybody would talk about it, saying how bogus it was that the little boy had gotten killed, but soon there would be another tragedy to get the hood's attention, and only the family would be left to grieve. The news would stop talking about it, no more flyers about a reward for the killers, no more tearful requests for the murderers to turn themselves in, the city would clean up any memorials and the prayer vigils would stop. In the end, the boy would join a long list of innocent people gunned down in Chicago.

Tutu ran his fingers lightly across his bullet wounds, a habit he had formed of late. The holes were developing nicely into scars, scars that would always remind him of the day he died several times. As a test, he drew the longest, deepest breath he could muster, and held it for as long as he could. He coughed a bit when he released it, but at least his lungs were filling up correctly. His mind went to the steroid inhaler he'd been prescribed, but he declined to use it unless it was totally necessary.

After pouring himself a cup of ice water from the container on his tray table, he took a seat. As he crunched a mouthful of ice, he realized that going home also meant no more hospital ice; he would miss that. He would definitely miss the nice nursing staff here. The doctors were mostly all business, maybe cracking a corny joke or two, but ready to get on with their rounds. The nurses and the CNAs were there 24/7 taking care of anything you might need. He knew they were just doing their jobs, but it felt good to have someone take care of you like they did.

That made him think of his mother, Meeka. Meeka had always taken care of his material needs like clothes, shoes, food and shelter and he was grateful for that, but she never really tended to Tyrese or his emotional needs. It was all surface with Meeka, you couldn't get to talking about feelings or get too deep or she would shut down on you or leave the room. He really couldn't even recall her crying over Tyrese, though he knew for a fact she loved him. He thought to deal with her pain, she just stayed drunk. Every minute she could she was drinking, on her way to get a drink or already drunk. For the first time since he could remember, Meeka was starting to look old too,

especially when standing next to her identical twin
Neeka. Meeka had been a teen parent; she had Tyrese
at 16 and him at 18. She had always been young and
pretty to him, but lately she looked older and tired. If
it wasn't for his auntie Neeka, he would never know
his mother Meeka had a story to tell, though she
wouldn't tell it herself. His aunt was the one that told
him about his father. The same father that didn't show
up to his own son's funeral. According to his aunt, his
daddy Tyrone, was the reason Meeka didn't show her
emotions to this day.

When his father met his mother she was 15 years
old and he was 22 years old and married. Neeka told
him that his daddy lied about being married and his
age to Meeka. Supposedly his father was handsome
and making a lot of money from selling crack in
those days, so he attracted plenty of young girls.
Though she was young, plenty of boys and men in the
neighborhood paid attention to the twins, Shameeka
and Shaneeka. They were both fair-skinned with long
hair and shapely bodies for their age. His father Tyrone
had a crush on Meeka and pursued her relentlessly.
She got pregnant by him at 15 and again at 18 with
several abortions in between.

The story went that he left his wife for Meeka, but
Neeka said his wife left him. His mother and father got
an apartment together after he was born. Neeka said
she never saw signs that Tyrone was beating her, but she
knew for a fact that he constantly verbally abused her.
Long ago he turned Meeka against their grandmother,
Nan that raised them. Meeka and Neeka's mother had
died of a stroke brought on by overdosing on crack
in the early 90s. Since their grandmother always had

them most of the time, she just kept the twins after their mother passed.

Auntie Neeka said she hated seeing her twin so head over heels about an obviously no-good man, so she always argued with and cussed Tyrone out. Once he and Meeka got their apartment together, Tyrone made sure Neeka and any of their family and friends knew they weren't welcome there. Though Tyrone would cheat on Meeka and treat her like dirt, she loved him more than she loved herself. Neeka said Tyrone even tried to get with her several times pretending like he didn't know the difference between her and her sister, but when she told Meeka, she wouldn't believe it.

Neeka stopped coming around their apartment, but she would still babysit her nephews all the time to make sure Nan and the rest of the family got to know them. Eventually Tyrone ended up getting caught for dealing drugs and wound up in prison for ten years. In the beginning, Neeka said Meeka would dress Tyrese up and ride for hours to see Tyrone in the penitentiary, while leaving him with Neeka because he was so small. On those visiting days, Meeka would bump into all sorts of women coming to see Tyrone, and even found out about several more children he'd fathered during the time they were together.

Tutu knew that he must really be in his feelings if he was thinking about his father. He never thought about his father, he actually had to remind himself that he had one. He knew he had plenty of brothers and sisters, but he didn't know any of them so in his mind, Meeka, Neeka and his cousins were all the family he had in this world. His aunts on his father's side would try to reach out to him through Meeka, but in his mind he just didn't see the point. When Tyrese died they came around a couple of times, but that didn't last long.

It didn't last too long with anyone he realized and pretty soon, he and Meeka were all alone. Now that he thought about it, when he went home tomorrow he would be alone again, for a while anyway. He got up to pour himself another cup of ice water when a member of the hospital transportation staff walked into his room, pushing a facility wheelchair.

"Mr. Young, don't sit on the bed, have a seat in my chair," said Tremont, the guy from transportation. Tremont rolled the wheelchair nearer to Tutu and put the brakes on as he waited for him to climb aboard. Once he was seated, Tremont swung him around and pushed him out of the room to make their way to the elevators.

"So, they tell me you're about to blow this popsicle stand," Tremont said cheerfully. "That's good, young brother. Real good. I'm happy for you."

"Yeah thanks," Tutu said, and he couldn't help it, because it came out almost as sad as he felt.

CHAPTER 9

Tutu stood in the kitchen in front of the stainless steel microwave waiting on his pizza rolls to heat up. He had already poured himself a large cup of Pepsi, leaving only an ounce or so of the caramel colored soda in the plastic two liter bottle he'd put back in the refrigerator. As he was waiting on the microwave to ping, his 7-year old cousin, Eric Jr or EJ as they called him, walked into the kitchen. He looked over at his chubby, spoiled cousin with a look of disgust before returning his attention to the microwave.

"What you doing, Tutu?" EJ inquired innocently.

"I'm minding my own business," he answered. "You need to find you some and leave mines alone."

EJ ignored his remark as he squeezed past him and stood on his toes to peer into the microwave. "Oooouuuuu! I want some pizza rolls, Tutu. Tutu give me some pizza rolls."

Tutu scowled. "Nall boy, I ain't giving you none of these. You just ate. Gone head on EJ."

"I'm still hungry," EJ complained. "That food wasn't nothing, I still want something to eat. I'm gone tell my daddy you won't give me none of your pizza rolls."

"I don't give a…" Tutu started, but caught himself.

"I don't care boy. Tell yo daddy. I'm gone tell Neeka you was begging and she told you about that. Plus you keep bothering me and you still trying to eat."

EJ stood there with his lips poked out and his arms folded across his little husky chest. Tutu ignored him as he waited for his food to heat completely. When the microwave pinged he took his pizza rolls and cup of pop and left the kitchen, followed closely by EJ. He went into the living room where his older cousin, Quincy, was in the recliner talking to his bucktooth girlfriend on Facetime. Que, as they called him, was brushing his waves as usual while he talked.

Que was two years older than Tutu and a star football and baseball player at Thornton, the local high school. Tutu liked his muscular, older cousin even though they didn't have much in common. Que never went outside and for the life of him, he couldn't understand that. If he wasn't at school or one of his many games, Que was in the house. To Tutu it was so crazy to him that a boy as popular as his cousin was with the school girls, only had eyes for his little, bucktooth girlfriend named Pierce. As Tureon took a seat on the loveseat and put his cup on the end table, EJ sat next to him.

"You really ain't gone give me no pizza rolls, Tutu?" EJ whined.

"Leave me alone," Tutu said evenly. "You just ate a Whopper and onion rings when Neeka dropped you off a little while ago. You ain't even hungry, you just want it 'cause you see it."

"You coulda had Burger King too," EJ countered.

"I don't eat that, that's why I'm eating this," he explained with way more patience than he felt. "Gone now and quit trying to finesse my pizza rolls boy."

Tutu really couldn't stand EJ or his father Eric, his aunt Neeka's boyfriend. He really couldn't understand for the life of him, how someone as cool as his aunt Neeka had a guy like Eric for a boyfriend. When he was released from the hospital two months ago he thought he was going home, but his mama and auntie had different plans. Instead of going back to Meeka's apartment on Gray Street, he was deposited at Neeka's house in Lansing, a suburban city outside of Chicago.

It was a really nice, ranch style house and the neighborhood was quiet, and it would have been an ideal setting to recuperate in, but he couldn't stand Neeka's boyfriend Eric. He was a short, crybaby of a man that never stopped complaining; that's all he did was complain. His mother Meeka said of Eric, if you put him in Heaven he would find something to complain about. He also knew that Eric didn't want him here, as much as he didn't want to be there.

Whenever he was in earshot and his aunt wasn't around, Eric would be mumbling little slick stuff directed at Tureon under his breath. He was always grumbling about, 'his food, his electricity, his air conditioning, his house'. He made sure he didn't show any of that negative energy when Neeka was around though. It had gotten worse in the last couple of weeks and by now he was really on his nerves; it was enough to make him want to call Meeka and tell her to come get him. It had gotten so bad, he had even tried walking. Walking served several purposes; it helped him to cool off, he got to explore the neighborhood and it helped rebuild his stamina.

The downside of his walking was he quickly found out there wasn't much to do in Lansing, especially without a car. To make matters worse, whenever he talked to any of his friends back in the city, they made it seem like every day was so lit and that he was missing so much. When he called, he would try to stay on the phone with his friends for a while, but after a few moments, Vah or Tree or whoever would be rushing him off the phone. He was missing Misha too. They texted and talked all the time, and she had even come out here twice when her older sister let her borrow the car. He didn't know how she did it, but she was looking better every time he saw her. Between missing home, his homies and Misha, he had had his fill of Lansing, though he didn't want to disappoint Meeka or Neeka.

Tutu bit into a pizza roll, but it was too hot so he spit it out onto his plate. He sat his plate of pizza rolls on the edge of the coffee table to give them time to cool off and took a big gulp of Pepsi. EJ eyed his plate hungrily.

"Tutu, you really ain't gone give me none?" EJ asked miserably.

"Nall boy, gone head on begging. Que get yo brother, man."

Que stopped brushing his hair long enough to say, "EJ, go find you something to do and leave Tutu alone."

EJ huffed and puffed as he refolded his arms and poked his bottom lip out even further. Tutu gave him a contempt filled glare. In his mind he thought, this is exactly what I'm talking about. If I was at the crib with just me and Meeka, I wouldn't be dealing with this little fat, greedy spoiled goofy, or his lame ass daddy.

It was Meeka and Neeka's plan that he stay for the summer and enroll in the high school there in the fall.

Meeka was going to save all the money she could and move out here by the time he was 17 and then he could move back with her. He already knew that plan wasn't going to work; it was just barely May and he was past ready to go home. He hoped Meeka wouldn't be mad, at least he had given it a try. He knew Neeka was gone trip though, she was the one he would have to get past. As much as he loved his auntie, he just wasn't cut out for living here. He missed the block, his gang and his home too much. Plus he didn't want whoever shot him up to think it was over or that he was scared. Really, he was ready to get back in the field and get his lick back for his brother and for himself.

"Tutu, just let me get a couple, pretty please," EJ begged. "I swear I won't ask you for anything else."

"Really EJ? I done said no like 20 times, what's wrong with you?"

"I'm hungry!" EJ shouted. "You can give me some and go make you some more."

"This is crazy," Tutu said. "Man gone…"

With what he thought was lightning quick speed, EJ reached over and snatched two handfuls of pizza rolls off of Tutu's plate and jumped up to make his getaway. He took two steps and before Tutu had a chance to react, EJ's flip-flop got caught on the edge of the rug and he pitched forward face first into the coffee table. The pizza rolls spilled from one of his hands, but the other handful he squeezed. So tight in fact they burst in his hand, filling his palm with scalding hot cheese, meat and sauce.

"That's what yo fat butt get," Tutu said laughingly. "God don't like ugly."

Embarrassed, EJ hurriedly got to his feet and started

crying from the pain in his hand. As he stood there shaking the smashed pizza rolls off of his hand, Tutu laughed heartily causing Que to crack a smile at his little brother's dilemma, that is until a trickle of blood ran down EJ's forehead. Both Tutu and Que looked at the blood on EJ's face, seconds before EJ felt it. He put his hand to his forehead and when he brought it down there was blood on it. He lost his mind and started hollering at the top of his lungs like someone was trying to kill him.

Eric Sr. was in the garage attached to the house wiping down his car when he heard EJ's distress calls. He dropped his rag and went to see why his baby boy was yelling at the top of his lungs. Neeka was in the laundry room downstairs when she heard the commotion. She finished loading the machine and set the cycle to start it before heading up the stairs to find out what was going on with EJ.

Eric entered the living room and surveyed the scene. He looked over at EJ. "What are you crying for?" he asked sharply. "What are you crying for EJ?"

EJ staggered over to Eric like he'd just been knifed in a pool hall brawl. He held out his hand showing the blood on it. "Daddy, Tutu burnt my hand and made me bust my head just because I wanted some of his pizza rolls."

By this time, Neeka had entered the living room too. She took EJ's hand and examined it, the skin was irritated but it wasn't burnt. She took a look at his forehead, wiping the blood off with the hem of her shirt. She saw the cut wasn't deep or wide, and wouldn't require any stitches.

"Do he need stitches?" Eric asked in an annoyed

voice.

"Ain't nothing but a scratch," she said to EJ. "He'll be alright."

Eric turned on Tutu. "Why you do that to my son?"

Tureon scowled. "I ain't do nothing to him. He snatched my food off my plate and tried to run and tripped. He hit his own head, I ain't touch him. He shouldn'ta snatched my food."

"No, he snatched my food," Eric said nastily. "You ain't got no food around here. I buy the food in this house. I don't spend stamps neither. That ain't Link, that's my hard-earned cash. So remember that, you don't buy food, you just eat it."

"Wwwoooowwwww!!!!!" Tutu said. "Tell me how you really feel."

"What you say boy," Eric asked as he moved closer to Tureon. Neeka tried to hold him back, but he pushed her hands off of him. "Nall, nall. Move Neeka. Tutu need to hear this. First of all you watch yo mouth, you ain't never finta disrespect me under my roof. This is my house! And just so you know, this is EJ house and that's food I buy for him, not you. So if he want some of yo food, then you better give him some."

It was Tutu's turn to come forward. "What you say? Who you think you talking to?"

Que saw how quickly things had escalated so he got off the couch and moved with the speed and grace of a champion athlete, as he slid between his cousin and his stepdad. He was far stronger than both of them, so he easily pushed them apart and held them at arm's length from one another. "Nall, Que. Move cuz. I'm tired of him, he been picking with me since I came here."

That was news to Neeka's ears. "What? What you do to my nephew, Eric?"

"I ain't do nothing to him. I just ain't like the way he was walking around my house like we sposed to be scared of big, bad Tutu, so I said something. Told him to bring it down some, this ain't the hood. I can say something to him in my house. Who is he? He ain't no egg, ain't nobody gone break him if they say something to him. I just didn't want him to be no bad influence on EJ or Que. Plus I pay the bills around here, I can say what I want to say around here, this is my house."

"Boy, you woofin, this my auntie house," Tutu said viciously. "She had it before she even knew who you was. Her and Que daddy bought this house, so you can quit fronting yo move."

"Be quiet Tutu," Neeka said. She turned to EJ and asked, "Now why in the hell is you snatching food off of someone's plate, like you ain't never ate before?"

"He said I could have it," EJ lied. "When I got it, he tripped me and made me hit my head."

"Boy you is lying!" Tutu exclaimed. "Why is you lying?"

"I done already told you about raising your voice in my house, Tutu. My son ain't got to lie on you. You the liar!"

Tutu's face turned red with rage as he tried to get past Quincy. He wanted to move Que's arm, but he couldn't budge it. "Let me go, Que. I'll show you lying, Eric. Let me go."

"Calm down, Tutu," Neeka ordered.

"Yo guy tweaking, auntie! EJ straight lying. I ain't tell him he could have my food, he snatched it!"

"Boy if you don't stop hollering at my woman you

better, I ain't gone ask you no more, I'm gone put my hands on you," Eric threatened.

Tutu lost it. "Then what, if you touch me I'm gone air yo ass out. I bet you don't put yo hands on nobody else fam after I pop you."

Eric turned to Neeka. "You heard him baby!" he shouted. "He just threatened to shoot me! That's it, he gotta go! I said he could stay 'til he was healed, he healed enough to say he gone shoot me, then he healed enough to go home. Today!"

Before Neeka could reply, Tutu said, "I don't care. I been ready to go home, what is you talking about. Auntie, please take me home before I be in jail, 'cause if he put his hands on me, I'm gone wet his ass up. I'm finta go get my stuff Neeka. I ain't trying to hear what Meeka was talking about neither. I ain't finta stay in this house with him here one more night, take me to the crib auntie."

Without waiting for Neeka to respond, Tutu turned on his heels and left the living room. He went to the guest bedroom to pack his things. As he was collecting his items, Neeka and Quincy came into the room. Quincy was rolling his basketball around in his hands as Neeka leaned against the door.

"You know you don't have to leave, Tutu," Neeka said. "Give Eric a minute to calm down, then apologize. Que already told him EJ was lying and that it was all his doing."

Tutu stopped stuffing his clothes into his bag. "I ain't apologizing to that lame. He got me messed up Auntie. He been saying slick stuff out his mouth since I got here. I love you, Auntie and I appreciate what you did for me. Que, you know you always good with me cuzo, but as for EJ and Eric, I'm straight on both of them."

"But that don't mean you should give up, Tutu," Quincy said. "The family love you and want to make sure you good cuz."

"I'll be good cuz," Tutu said as he returned to packing. "It's time Que. I'ma be alright."

"So we can't change your mind. Tutu?" Neeka asked.

"Not on this one Auntie. Like ole boy said, I was just supposed to be here until I healed. Guess what? I'm healed, it's time to go home."

Neeka walked over to her nephew and gave him a hug. "Well, Tutu, regardless of what Eric said, you have a place to go as long as I got a home. If you just need some time away from the hood, promise me that you'll come out here, if for nothing but to clear your mind. Promise me that."

Tutu nodded his head.

"That ain't good enough, Tutu," Neeka said. "I need to hear you say you promise. Promise me, if you're ever in trouble, need a place to stay or you're just trying to get away for a while, you'll come to my home."

"I promise, Auntie," he said. "I know you're my other mother. Just promise me that when I come, your boyfriend won't say nothing to me."

"I promise," Neeka replied. "I just gotta grab my purse and I'll be in the car. I really didn't feel like going into the city, but oh well. I might as well get me some Harold's chicken while I'm there."

CHAPTER 10

Tutu came out of the bathroom at home. His cell phone was in his hand and it was on speakerphone as he waited for the person he'd called to pick up. Instead of his party answering the call went to voicemail. He started to hang up, but decided against it and left a message.

"Tree, this Tutu, gang. Hit my line when you get the message. The first video shoot is today and I'm trying to let you know the locay, so you can link. Bump my line bro."

Tutu hung up the phone as his mother, Meeka walked past on her way to the kitchen. She was going to use the stove to light the cigarette dangling from her mouth because she couldn't find her lighter. She fanned the air with her hand as she walked past him and the bathroom.

"Damn, Tutu, yo ass stink boy!" she exclaimed. "Spray some air freshener with yo stinky self. You need to drink more water boy."

He grinned. "Gone nah, Meeka. It ain't sposed to smell like flowers when you take a dump."

"Boy that wasn't no dump that was toxic waste. And I know you got my lighter. Give me back my lighter."

"I ain't got yo lighter OG, you capping. Go look in that big purse of yours or that junky car."

"Let me find out you got my lighter," Meeka said as she continued on to the kitchen. "Pull that bathroom door closed too."

Tutu went into his bedroom and sat on his bed, taking extra care not to wrinkle the new clothes laid out on his bed. He sat for a moment, then got up and began to practice the lyrics to the song they would be recording a video for today, in the mirror on the back of the closet door.

He had always wanted to be a rapper, and while he was in the hospital, he'd started writing lyrics in his phone. Bars came easy to him and before he knew it he had compiled a lot of songs and freestyles verses. When he was staying with his Aunt Neeka, on his many long walks he would practice his lyrics and delivery. No one knew of his hidden talent, not Meeka, his closest friends, no one. He knew he was good, especially compared to the level of talent being pushed in the city right now. It was premature, but he was already dreaming of cars, women, money and jewelry.

In the weeks since he'd moved back home with Meeka, he was biding his time, just waiting for the right moment to show his guys what he could do. While he was in Lansing, the big homie Geno, had gotten ahold of a studio, though he didn't have a musical bone in his body. Geno was a hustler, so when the former owner gave him the studio to settle a drug debt, he did some remodeling and opened it for business. Geno was always at the studio, so he started going there and hanging out, trying to get a feel for the place he felt would one day be his second home.

Often when they were at the studio, they would just get high and listen to any artists recording that day. Tutu was still waiting on what he felt would be the right moment. The event that lit a fire under him was when a rapper from the 8 Deuces named Pioneer mentioned his brother Tyrese's name in one of his songs. In the song he was dissin members of Gray Street Gang when he said that he was smoking on a Tyrese blunt, an extremely disrespectful comment.

In response to that track, he wrote a harsh diss verse aimed at Pioneer and all 8 Deuce Hotheads. This time he felt he was ready to record, but he was scared to ask Geno so a couple of more days passed. One night when he was chilling in the studio with Tree, Geno, Danno, Vah, Pooh, and the studio's in-house producer Freethrow, he asked to get in the booth. Everyone thought he was joking, but Geno sensed that he was serious. Tutu told them he wanted to record an answer to Pioneer's record.

"Put the beat on to Pioneer's record," Geno instructed Freethrow. "Shorty, you ready?"

"Yeah," he said as he walked into the booth. He closed the door behind himself and walked over to the mic. He put on a pair of headphones hanging there, and felt a surge of adrenaline as the music filtered into his ears.

"Turn my headphones up a little," Tutu said, mimicking the many rappers he'd heard say this before. "Turn them up a little bit more. Alright, that's good." He let the beat rock in his ears as he built up adrenaline, and just when everyone in the studio thought he wasn't going to do anything, he snapped. Bar after crisp bar he recited with plenty of punchlines that landed with deadly force as he spit them with his deliberate delivery. Everyone in the studio thought he might sound somewhat okay. Some of them even thought he was just playing around, but as his lyrics unfolded, they watched and listened in awe. They all realized he was dope as hell on the mic.

To him it felt so good to release the words that had been pent up inside of him for all this time. "Goofies thought they got me/ thought I was gone snitch cause y'all popped me/ you didn't stop me/ only made me more cocky/ lucky for you I didn't have my Glock gee/ after this you gone block me/ I'm gone have yo baby mama knock me/Pioneer you mad cause you fat and sloppy/and yo wifey be on top of me/ if I was a crispy pair of Vapormax Pioneer couldn't rock me/you too old to be all in yo videos trying to wop B/yo gun ain't real it's a prop gee…"

Tutu finished his verse and took off the headphones and returned them to the hook without much flair. As he walked out of the booth, all of them just stared at him. One of the rappers Geno managed, a kid named Pekoe had also come into the studio while Tutu was in the booth, and was openly staring at him with admiration for his mic skills.

Pekoe spoke first. "Damn, Tutu you just went brazy in the booth. Them yo rhymes?"

"Yeah," he answered with a look that said who else rhymes would they be.

"My bad. No disrespect, gang," Pekoe said in an apologetic tone. "It's just I see you around here all the time, and I ain't have no idea you was nasty like that on the mic."

"Nobody did!" Vah interjected as he jumped up out

of his seat to show his homie some love. "This my day one and I ain't know. Damn, Tutu you just set the booth on fire. My boy got bars. You heard him, Tree?"

"Yeah, I heard him," Tree said without much enthusiasm.

Danno walked over to Tutu and showed him some love with the Gray Street Gang handshake. "My boy, man Tyrese would be super proud of you bro. You got his lick back too. Geno what you think, big homie?"

Geno looked up from his cell phone. "Lil Tyrese you got wit em on that verse. I liked it, but anybody can spit a freestyle verse. Can you write a song though?"

"Yeah, I can," Tutu said confidently as he pulled his cell phone out of his pocket. "I got songs already done."

Geno shook his head. "Nall, nall. Most dudes can sit somewhere, kick they feet up and write. I want somebody that can put a song together anywhere and anytime."

"I can do that," Tutu reassured Geno.

"Yeah?" Geno asked. "Freethrow give the little homie a beat, let's see what he can do. Get you one of those pens and pads from over there on the shelf."

Freethrow spun around in his chair and took a hard drive from his backpack. He plugged in the drive and keyed up its contents. Tutu took a seat next to him as he began playing snippets of beats. On the eighth track, Tutu stopped him.

"Freethrow, let me hear that beat again."

Freethrow let the beat rock for Tutu and soon he was nodding his head to the music.

"That's it, that the track," he announced. "Email me that bro."

"That track go crazy Tutu," Pekoe said. "If you don't want it, I do."

"You get it, Tutu?" Freethrow asked.

"Yeah, it just came through. Thanks." As he was downloading the track to his phone, Tutu collected the pad and pen and went to take a seat on the futon couch in the corner of the room. He listened to the track a few times and began to write. About ten minutes passed and he called Pekoe over to him and they both began writing on the pad. Tree pretended not to notice, but he was watching them intensely.

Geno, Vah, Danno and Pooh began playing Spades as they smoked blunts and drank Hennessey. Tree watched the card game as he kept an eye on Tutu and Pekoe. Freethrow was working on a new track and sipping some Patron at the boards. The Spades game had grown loud and boisterous when Tutu and Pekoe suddenly stood up.

"We done," Tutu proclaimed as they walked over to Freethrow. "Pekoe on the hook with me, we ready to lay this down."

Freethrow looked over at Geno questioningly. Geno gave him the nod of approval and swept his arm in the direction of the booth. Pekoe followed Tutu inside and they both put on headphone sets. Freethrow keyed up the beat and pointed at the pair of rappers through the glass. They got down to business as Pekoe started off with the hook of the song and Tutu followed him with the first verse. By the time they got to the hook again everybody in the studio was dancing around, except Freethrow and Tree. Tree stood off to the side with a look born of envy and jealousy on his face.

When the song was finished the pair of rappers left

the booth, and this time Tutu didn't have to wait for their responses. Even Geno who was usually either menacing or laid back was excited as they all congratulated the both of them. Freethrow just kept saying, "That's a hit. That's a hit." They all gathered around showing love with the GSG handshake, but when it was Tree's turn to show love, he gave Tutu a weak handshake, and acted like he didn't see Pekoe's outstretched hand. Before Tutu had a chance to question his homie about his weird energy, Geno put his arm around his shoulders.

"Tutu, you tough on that mic, little homie. I been looking for a artist my Savage Life Records could really get behind. On God, Tutu, you even got Pekoe sounding better. What you think about dropping a couple of singles on my label?"

He grinned as he said, "That sound good, big homie."

"Well, I'm gone make sure you get in yo bag. You just gotta do what you need to do for the team and we gone get on for real."

"What you need me to do?" asked Tutu as he rubbed his hands together Bird Man style, "Because I shole need some bread."

Geno thought for a second. "The first thing I'ma need you to do is finish that Pioneer diss record. Write another verse or two to that, lay it down and we'll be shooting a video for it in a couple of days. We can get some buzz going around that, get yo views up, then wham hit em with Let It Ride. After that I guarantee you, you doing shows. From there, you on yo way to the bag. If you serious I'll show you how serious I am."

"Say yeah Tutu, because I'm gone be yo hype man," Vah said seriously.

"I'm toting the bangers bro," Danno proclaimed. "I'ma be on point."

"Hell yeah," Pooh added as he shook hands with Danno. "I'm on that too, you gone need shooters on deck, bro. 'Specially when you doing shows."

"Right now, I need Pekoe to get in the booth and tighten up the hook and put some more ad-libs on it," Geno said. "Tutu, smoke you a blunt, take you a shot and get ready to finish up that Pioneer diss."

Following his new boss's instructions, Tutu took a blunt from the table and poured himself a shot of Hennessey from the bottle. He wanted to make a call so he stepped out on the back porch of the studio by going through a pair of sliding glass doors. As he lit his blunt he speed-dialed his mother Meeka so he could tell her the good news. Meeka didn't answer so he figured he'd talk to her in the morning. Before he could step back inside the studio, the door opened and Tree stepped out onto the back porch too.

"Tree, wassup bro, you good?" he asked.

"Not really," Tree replied.

"Hunh? What's popping bro?"

Tree didn't answer at first, then he exploded, "How you gone put Pekoe on that song? You don't even know buddy like that, plus he weak as hell. You know I could have done that hook, I been rapping. We sposed to be gang."

"Man, get yo ass outta here, you can't rap," Tutu said with a dismissive laugh. "We is gang and I ain't never heard you rap before. Boy, you can't even stay on beat when you rapping somebody else song. You is tweaking, Pekoe good, he wrote that hook and hit it just right. Stop cappin."

"Tutu you cappin, I'm good. All of that don't make no difference, you the one ain't showing no loyalty. How you gang gang and you letting somebody eat before yo bro?"

He realized now that Tree was serious. "You for real for real hunh? Man, Pekoe is gang too, bro is GSG all day. Plus you ain't never said nothing about you wanted to make no music, so how the hell was I spose to know you wanted to do something? And how I got somebody eating when I ain't even eating yet?"

"You finta be," Tree retorted. "Geno was saying while you was in the booth that he finta make sure you get in yo bag."

"That's dope," Tutu said with a big smile, then he remembered how his friend was feeling. "Look bro, I ain't know you wanted to make music. I ain't never trying to leave my homie behind. I'm finta go in there and holla at Geno right now. You got some of yo rhymes with you?"

Tree nodded. "In my phone."

"You got something that can go on that Pioneer record?"

Tree thought about it for a moment. He shrugged his shoulders. "I should."

"Okay, this is what I'm thinking, I'm gone see if Pekoe got some bars for it too, and y'all two can get on it too. You can do the last verse too, you just gotta make sure you go in. That's Gucci?"

"Yeah, that's cool," Tree answered.

He handed Tree the blunt. He said, "Well c'mon, I'm finta holla at Geno real quick."

Back in the studio, Tutu pulled Geno to the side and had a quick conversation with him. Everything must have been favorable because he went to Pekoe next and after a few words with him, Pekoe headed for the recording booth. Tutu was coming back over to talk to Tree, while Geno was telling Freethrow to key up the beat to the Pioneer diss record.

"Get ready bro, you next, unless you need some time," Tutu told Tree.

"I'm straight," Tree said. He pulled his cell phone from his pocket. He went over to the side to practice, but mainly he ended up watching and listening to Pekoe.

It took Pekoe a few takes, but he eventually grabbed hold of the beat and went haywire on it with some serious bars. Freethrow made him go back and double up his vocals, and place his ad libs on the track. When he was finished, Pekoe emerged from the recording booth to handshakes and hugs. Tutu looked at Tree and nodded his head in the direction of the recording booth. Tree wasn't looking too confident as he walked to the booth. He looked more like a man going to the gas chamber than going to record his lyrics for a song in a studio recording booth.

Pekoe noticed Tree's look of reluctance to enter the booth. He said, "Good luck bro. I know it's hard to come behind so much heat, but you gone be good. Well not as good as me, but then again who is."

Tree scowled at him and gave him the middle finger salute as he walked past. Semi-confidently, he said, "Watch and learn fam. My bars gone sound better because I ain't making mine up. I'm real, you make believe."

Inside the booth Tree adjusted a pair of headphones on his ears and stepped to the mic. He looked out the booth at Freethrow and pointed to him. Freethrow cued up the track, but from the very start Tree had problems staying with the beat as he tried to rhyme. He stopped and started time after time as he asked for the mic and the headphones to be turned up because he couldn't hear himself. Next he said it was hot in the booth, and he needed some water because his mouth was dry. Take after take, he fumbled and stumbled through his lyrics mostly being offbeat on each one of them.

At the studio boards, Freethrow looked over at Geno and shrugged. Geno, however, remained stone-faced. By the 17th take, Tree was so frustrated he snatched the earphones off of his head and stormed out of the recording booth.

"Man, I can't even catch that wack ass beat," Tree complained. "You sure that's the beat Tutu was on? That can't be, it don't even sound the same. Do it? Let me just get another beat. Something that ain't wack like that Pioneer beat. They should throw the whole beat away."

There was an awkward silence in the studio as most of Tree's friends avoided eye contact with him. Geno chose to be silent as he let the smoke from the blunt he was smoking curl around his head.

Finally he said, "We ain't doing that young homie. That's the same beat both of them boys just got on and destroyed. That was Tutu's track and if he wanted you on it, that's on him, but if you want another track, beats cost money. Didn't nobody else have no problem with the track."

"Yeah that was easy," Pekoe chimed in with a grin on his face. "Me and Tutu smashed it. I don't see what the problem was bro."

Tree spun around on Pekoe, but Danno pushed him back. "Man little buddy, I wasn't talking to you," Tree said fiercely. "I'll be done…"

Pekoe lifted his shirt showing the handle of the pistol he was carrying, but the smile never left his face as, he said, "Somehow you got me messed up bro, but it's all good. Ask around they'll tell you, I minds my business, but not because nobody telling me to. Save that energy for the opps or the booth bro. I'm just here to make music."

Tree tried to push Danno out the way, but he couldn't.

"Man, who you think you talking to? Move Danno! Why is you holding me? You seen this boy just front his move like it's sweet. How we not taking that hammer from him and doing him dirty? Tutu, that's what you on? You let this goofy up his burner on me?"

"Tree, what is wrong with you boy?" Tutu asked. "You tweaking! You making that up, gang ain't even up his banger, he just showed you he got his heater on him while you trying to get aggressive for no reason. I don't know why you is even on that, ain't no opps in here, boy."

Tree stopped struggling with Danno and put his hands up in the air. "You know what Tutu? You right, I am tweaking. I see what's popping though. You riding with this clout chaser over me. Whole time that's crazy. I never would have believed Tutu from Gray Street would do me this greasy. We sandbox homies, but I guess you'll throw that away for money."

With a bewildered look on his face, Tutu asked, "Boy what is you even talking about? You must be superman high foolie. You need to leave them mids alone, them pills be having yo mind. You need to go home and sleep off whatever it is you on. Take you some time, practice yo lyrics and come back ready to lay it down. Simple as that."

"That's what I'm talking about Tutu. That boy bars was trash and you ain't said nothing. I ain't tweaking, I see what's happening. I'm straight though. I'm gone go somewhere else and record, this ain't the only studio. I aint finta be around all this hatin and dickriding."

Tree turned and moved in the direction of the exit. Tutu started to follow behind him, but Geno put his hand on his shoulder.

"Let him go," Geno said simply. "You don't want to believe it, but whole time that boy is jealous of you, mad because he can't do what you do. The best thing you can do is throw the whole friendship away."

"But that's gang," Tutu protested.

"The question ain't whether he gang or not," Geno said. "The question is whether he in the same gang. Just cause somebody call you bro, and throw up what you throw up, and come from the same set, don't make them gang. If he really gang, how he gone be mad at you having a opportunity to get in yo bag? Real gang like Vah and Pooh right here ain't tripping. Bro nem gone get in where they fit in, same thing Tree should be doing. You better get ready Tutu, because success brings the best and worst out of the people closest to you."

Tutu's shoulders sagged a bit as he admitted internally that Geno was right.

Geno added, "The best thing you can do for suckers like that, is move around from them. Now forget that boy, you need to write a couple more bars to end that up unless you wanna leave it like that."

That all happened six days ago and he hadn't heard from Tree. He'd called and sent text messages, but no answer.

He sighed as he thought, maybe Tree will stop tweaking and come around, or maybe he won't, but I can't focus on that right now. Tutu did his best to put Tree out of his head as he got dressed for his video shoot.

CHAPTER 11

Tutu was leaning back in a folding chair with his feet up on the banister on his porch. Pooh and Tree sat nearby on the concrete porch steps.

"Damn bro, where is yo weak ass weed man?" Tree asked with a scowl on his face. "You called homie like a half hour ago?"

"Yeah," Tutu replied, only half listening. He was busy checking the views and comments for the video of his diss of Pioneer's record. The video had exploded on the local music scene to the tune of nearly 500,000 hits on his Youtube channel in a little over a week.

The video was definitely an instant favorite with anybody claiming Gray Street Gang, and cars in the hood could be heard playing it as they drove past. Everyone didn't like it though, and it had inspired a weak response song from Pioneer that was being totally disregarded. Members of other gangs throughout the city had also made their own records, dissing Gray Street Gang, 8 Deuce and whomever, but none of them were as good as the song he'd made with Pekoe. There were thousands of comments on the video post too. On the strength of such a controversial song, Geno had managed to book him his first paid show tonight for $3,500, more money than he'd ever had in his life.

People all over had started to show their love for the song, but there was also plenty of hate. So far he had received plenty of online death threats. People that lived outside of Chicago were going so hard about the song it amazed him at first. Some of them had never seen Gray Street or 8 Deuce, but that didn't stop them from threatening him, his mother and his unborn children. To make matters worse, the disrespect they showed his brother's memory almost gave him a headache it made him so mad at first. Now though he was beginning to take it in stride as he realized most of them commenting were far removed from the war going on in the Chicago streets. He had heard about keyboard gangsters all his life, but had never been the victim of so many of them until now. When he talked to Geno about it, the big homie simply said, 'make music, not memes'.

He hadn't wanted to admit it that Geno was right at first, and he'd previously planned to answer each and every negative comment, but he saw quickly that that could become a never-ending job. Instead he chose to focus his energy on his music, though from time to time he would scroll through them for fun. His phone alerted that he had an incoming text message.

Misha: hit yo line later jus clockd in at work

Misha: jus wantd 2 say congrats on the show n good luck

Tureon: thanx when u get off slide

Misha: gone be 2 tired

Tureon: punk

Misha: gangbanger

Tureon: u like it

Misha: whatever bye boi do good tonite

Tureon: copy that

"Man, where this weed man at?" Tree inquired angrily. "That's why they be getting they ass robbed. They always talking about they on the pull up, but ain't pulled up yet. We need a new weed man."

We? Tutu thought. He knew that Tree never had any money to put up on the weed, or alcohol or pills, but he smoked and drank like he'd bought everything any chance he got.

Tree had just recently come back around and he suspected it was only to get high for free, because his attitude remained as messed up as it had always been. The big homie Geno, told him that he would respect that Tree was his homie, but to keep him away from him. Tutu felt him because lately, all Tree did was complain; even more than usual. Vah told Tutu that Tree saw the good time he'd missed on the day of the video shoot and that was the reason he came back around. Geno had really showed them a good time that day. There was plenty of money, guns, women, drugs and foreign cars on hand at the video shoot. If he knew Tree, he knew when Tree saw the video he was sick to his stomach about missing such a turn up. When he came back around Tree didn't apologize either, one day he wasn't around and the next day he was, simple as that. Tutu knew Tree felt the same way, because he'd caught him looking at Pekoe with a crazy look on his face more than once.

Knowing his friend, Tutu knew that Tree wanted to put his hands on Pekoe, but he knew Pekoe either had his gun on him or it was close at all times. Pekoe had also let Tutu know that he wouldn't hesitate to empty a clip into Tree.

"He ain't lying though," Pooh agreed. "These weed men is weak as hell. I bet if it was like pizza and yo weed was free if they take too long that'll make they ass hurry up."

"Boy y'all capping, this ain't Jimmy John's," Tutu commented.

"For real for real, where that man at?" Pooh asked. "I gotta go to the crib and change, I ain't wearing this to yo show."

"I bet you wish you still lived around here," Tree teased. "Got to get yo goofy ass on the bus."

"Difference is, I ain't scared to get on the bus, like some people," Pooh retorted.

Pooh's comment touched off another argument between him and Tree, which Tutu chose not to join in on. Instead he chose to ignore them and play a game on his cell phone. Tutu's head was in his game on his phone and Pooh and Tree were so busy arguing, none of them noticed the weed man's car pull up and park in front of the building. Inside the car, the weed man tapped the car horn to get their attention. Seeing who it was, Tutu hopped up out of his seat and jumped down the porch stairs. He got in the car, made the purchase and returned to the porch. They immediately started a smoke session by rolling a couple of blunts. A half hour later they were all high.

"C'mon y'all, walk me to the bus stop," Pooh said.

"You better gone boy, I ain't finta walk with you, I'm right here," Tree said seriously.

"Boy, you walking with us too," Tutu said. "I'm finta grab my pole then we can bounce."

Since he'd gotten shot, Tutu rarely went anywhere

without a gun. He went inside to get his gun and pulled on a yellow hoodie. He left out the apartment, taking care to lock the door behind him. On the porch, Tree and Pooh had sparked up another argument.

From his seat on the steps, Tree looked up at him. "Man, why you got that ugly yellow sweater on?"

Tutu ignored him and started down the steps.

"C'mon y'all."

As they started walking, Pooh explained the reason for their latest argument. "Look Tutu, yo boy Tree here is calling me a dick-rider because I like Pekoe music. I'm trying to tell his lame ass that only a real hater, hate somebody for no reason or because they think somebody is in they way."

"I don't think he in my way," Tree said. "If he was in my way, then I'd be on his heels. It ain't that I don't like him for no reason, I don't like him because I don't like him."

Pooh laughed. "Tutu, you hear this? Tree, you sound stupid as hell. He thinks because he doesn't like somebody is the reason to not like somebody. You slow as hell Tree."

Tree and Pooh continued to go back and forth as they crossed to the next block. As they were walking down the street an older model, red Jeep Cherokee drove slowly down the block. Unlike his two friends arguing, Tutu was alert and walking with his head on swivel so he noticed the SUV.

"Aye y'all shut up!" Tutu ordered. "On this red truck, they driving slow as hell."

His hand went to his gun as the truck was parallel to them. For a moment it looked like it was going to stop, but it kept going. They watched the Jeep as it drove to the corner and turned.

"That Jeep wasn't right yo," Tutu said warily.

"Boy, you tweaking, you think everybody the opps, that could be Uber eats," Tree said with a laugh.

"Yeah okay," Tutu said as they continued to walk. Before they reached the corner of the block, the same red Jeep Cherokee turned onto the block again.

Pooh spotted them first. "Here they come again. Look out! He got a gun!"

As the Jeep drew near and slowed down, a young guy with short dreads was hanging out of the window with a gun. The shooter must have gotten excited because he began shooting before they were in a good position, wasting his rounds. All six of his shots hit either parked cars, dirt or air. Before the Jeep could accelerate again Tutu popped up from behind the car he'd been hiding next to and shot several rounds at the vehicle. Two of his bullets thwacked into the side of the Jeep. The driver stepped on the gas and the tires burned rubber as the SUV peeled off. Tutu ran out in the street, blasting at the fleeing vehicle until his gun was empty.

Pooh jumped up from behind the car where he'd been hiding. Excitedly, he shouted, "Tutu, that's what's up bro! Air they ass out! Deuce killer!"

Brushing off his clothes as he got up out of the dirt where he'd dived on the ground, Tree complained, "Boy, you ain't even hit they ass. Tutu, yo fake famous ass almost just got us killed. Damn! My clothes is dirty now, how I'ma go to the show. You finta have to give me some of all them new clothes you got now."

Tutu cut Tree a look. "Boy you know you a bug," Tutu said as he unjammed his gun and put it back into the waistband of his pants. "You so irra. C'mon y'all, we outta here, y'all standing here like I didn't just air this block out."

The three boys jogged away and soon they were on the bus stop, laughing as they recounted the incident. The bus drove up and Pooh boarded it, promising to return as soon as he showered and changed his clothes. Once the bus pulled away from the stop, they began to walk back to Tutu's apartment.

As they walked, Tree demanded, "Tutu, I need some new clothes to put on. My outfit is messed up now. This is all yo fault, because of yo video all the opps know you now. You need to give me a fit, Geno bought you enough, you straight."

"You sound stupid bro," Tutu replied. "What's wrong with you? Sometimes I don't even know what to say to yo ass. I'll give you some clothes bro, just stop talking to me, bro. For real."

Tutu was so mad at Tree he started walking so fast, Tree had to jog to keep up. As they were about to cross the street a block later an unmarked police Ford Explorer flew across the intersection ahead of them. The police vehicle was across the street and headed for the next block when the driver slammed on the brakes and threw the vehicle into reverse.

"Be up bro!" Tutu shouted as he took off. He sprinted to the alley and dipped into it, there he ran through the first gangway that wasn't gated coming out on the next street. As he ran he heard footsteps behind him and looked over his shoulder expecting it to be the police, but it was Tree. ` "Quit following me!" Tutu breathed over his shoulder. "Gone boy!" He took off through another gangway, but Tree shadowed his every step. They dashed to the corner of the block and a Chicago Police blue and white Ford Explorer with its lights flashing screeched to a halt in front of them. Tutu cut to his left and went around the police vehicle like it wasn't there, but Tree ran into the side of the truck and bounced off of it. He landed on his back pockets and slid a bit. Before Tree could scramble to his feet, the policeman on the passenger side leapt from the vehicle and trained his weapon on Tree. "You bet not move a muscle boy!" the cop snarled.

Tree held up his hands as he watched Tutu scamper up the street. Tutu cut between two cars and fled across a vacant lot. As he ran his pants were falling, weighed down by his gun. He pulled his pants up with one hand and the gun slipped from his waistband. It clattered to the pavement in the middle of the street. He stopped on a dime and turned to retrieve his weapon, but from the corner of his eye, he saw a tall, skinny white cop in plain clothes running in his direction at full speed so he took off again. He led the tall policeman through gangways, yards and vacant lots, but he couldn't shake him. His lungs felt like sandpaper as he sucked wind. Instead of refreshing him, it felt like he was swallowing lava. He heard more and more sirens coming their way as he crossed another street. This time though, he misjudged the curb and tripped over it.

He tried to keep his balance, but he was so tired he couldn't right himself before face-planting in the grass there. Though he was the most tired he could ever recall being, he pushed himself up on his hands and knees, just in time for several policemen to start kicking and punching him into submission. The only thing he could do was curl himself into a ball while they beat him. His yellow hoodie was covered in footprints and dirt as they pounced on him and handcuffed him.

CHAPTER 12

Tutu sat alone in an interrogation room in the police station. The cinder block walls of the room had been painted a dark, drab gray and there weren't decorations of any kind on them. He sat in an ancient, wooden straight back chair at an iron leg table with a wooden top. Numerous names and gang signs had been scratched into the wooden table over the course of who knew how many years. Directly across from the table was a large two-way mirror.

He'd sat for the better part of what felt like two hours to him, staring at the mirror with a defiant look on his face. He tried not to show it, but his head and body were hurting like hell from being punched and kicked. He was also tired from getting high and then from being chased. As his adrenaline subsided it made him sleepy, so he decided to put his head down for a few moments and rest his eyes. He wasn't trying to sleep, just recharge his battery and gather himself, but soon his breathing grew regular as he fell asleep. On the other side of the mirror in the small room which was nestled in between two interrogation rooms, Gang Crimes Unit Detectives Millsap and Barrows watched him fall asleep. They had been watching him as they drank bitter police station coffee and talked about last night's Crosstown Classic baseball game between the Cubs and White Sox. It was a tactic of theirs to let a suspect rest a bit, then charge into the room waking them. Usually the suspect would be off-guard and confused from having been in such a relaxed state, and sometimes they would make a mistake in their alibi or an admission of their guilt.

Detective Barrows, a medium build, light-skinned Black man, drained his coffee and shot the empty cup into a waste basket against the wall. He said, "Let's go wake our boy up."

Detective Millsap, the tall, white man that had chased Tutu down, jerked his thumb at the interrogation room opposite of his. He suggested, "No, let's see what this one over here has to say first. We may not even have to wake that one up."

Tree was in the other interrogation room, which had the same exact setup as the one Tutu was in, except the difference was tears were streaming down Tree's face as he looked around anxiously.

"Yeah that's our victim," Det. Barrows agreed. "He should be easy."

Detective Millsap pulled out his wallet and looked into it. "Barrows, you got a couple of singles for the vending machines? I think our buddy there could use something to snack on."

Barrows pulled a few bills from his pocket and handed them over. Millsap left the room and went to the vending machine cove. There he purchased a bag of chips, a candy bar and a can of pop. He collected the snacks and took them into Tree's interrogation room. When he entered the room, Tree hurriedly used his sleeves to wipe his eyes and face. The detective placed the snacks in front of Tree and took a seat across the table from him. He waited for Tree to compose himself. Millsap just sat there for a few minutes, watching Tree steal hungry glances at the snacks.

"Go ahead eat," Millsap said pleasantly. "We're sending someone out for burgers in a bit, so I'll make sure you get one and some fries. That's ok?"

"Yes," Tree answered with a sniffle. He ripped open the bag of Sour Cream and Onion Ruffles like he hadn't eaten in years and devoured them. Next he tore open the Payday candy bar and ate it quickly. He finished everything off by gulping the can of Coke, all of which took him only the space of a few minutes.

"You good now?" Detective Millsap asked.

"Yes, sir. Thank you."

"That's good, Forrest. I just want to ask you one question."

"About what? I don't know nothing sir. What do you want with me?"

Detective Millsap didn't answer right away. He smirked as he dug into his pocket and withdrew a pack of gum. He removed a stick from the pack, unwrapped it and placed it in his mouth. He returned the pack to his pocket without offering Tree a piece.

"Ain't you gone give me a piece of gum?" Tree asked.

"I don't give my gum to liars," Millsap replied.

"How I lie?"

"You just said that you don't know anything. You think we just chased y'all down for the hell of it? Don't insult my intelligence, Forrest. Or should I call you Tree?"

The fact that the detective knew his nickname blew

Tree's mind. He wondered how that could be, then he assumed Tutu must have told them. He didn't know once the gang detectives had his real name it was a simple enough matter to find him on social media.

"I ain't gotta talk to you," Tree said stubbornly. "I know my rights."

Detective Millsap made as if to leave. "Okay, that's cool Tree. I just wanted to hear your side of the story. I mean your buddy is already in the other room telling his side. The way it sounds, he gone be going home and you'll be staying, but if you want to keep quiet that's okay with me."

Tree sat forward. "What Tutu saying I did? I ain't do nothing, that was him."

"Well, Tutu said it was you. Right now we're just waiting on the state's attorney so we can formally arrest you. Since you're 17 now, you know where you're going right? Gladiator school in the County. I hope you can fight Tree, because that's all them young boys do up there, is fight all day and night."

"This bogus! I ain't even do nothing!" Tree exclaimed as his tears began to fall again. "That was Tutu shooting. They shot first and he shot back. I wasn't doing nothing, but walking my friend to the bus stop. Now I gotta go to the County for nothing? Tutu lying! He was shooting at them, not me!"

"Alright, alright, calm down, let me check something real quick," Det. Millsap said. He got up and left the room without ceremony, returning to the room where his partner was located.

"What you think Barrows?" Millsap asked, as he looked through the window at Tutu, who was still napping.

"I try not to think, Millsap. Patrol found the vehicle that was involved in the shooting. The red truck in question turns out to be a 2003 Jeep Cherokee. It was reported stolen two days ago and the shooters abandoned it today. It had a couple of fresh bullet holes in the side, but no blood inside the vehicle. I don't think our boy Tutu hit anybody. What are you thinking? Do you want to talk to Sleeping Beauty?"

"For what? We know our boy Tutu did it. Like the 911 caller said, the boy with the yellow sweatshirt was shooting. Tutu has on the yellow hoodie and he dropped the gun. We got no victims and the caller said the boys in the red truck shot first. Tree said the same thing. If we would have had a body, Tree would have testified, but without one his testimony only proves it was self-defense."

Detective Barrows said, "Yeah, well we got the gun so at least that's unlawful use of a weapon and we can tack on discharging a weapon in city limits, but I don't know if it'll stick without eyewitnesses. I'm going to go ahead and arrest him."

Detective Millsap nodded his head in approval and Barrows got up and went into the interrogation room where Tutu was sleeping. He walked over to him and kicked his chair.

"Wake up, boy you're under arrest," Barrows commanded. "Stand up."

Tutu stood up and stretched. As he did Detective Barrows took hold of one of his wrists and pulled out his handcuffs. He proceeded to cuff Tutu as he recited, "You have the right to remain silent. Anything you say can and will be used against you in a court of law. You have the right to an attorney, if you cannot afford an attorney, one will be appointed to you. Do you understand these rights as I have told them to you?"

"I guess," Tutu said.

"Yes or no, boy."

"Yeah," he said defiantly. "Now where you taking me?"

Det. Barrows put a hand on Tutu's shoulder and steered him from the room.

"Where you taking me, man?"

"First of all, it's Detective Barrows," Barrows corrected him as he squeezed the back of Tureon's neck roughly. "You're going into the squad room so I can do your paperwork, after that you're going to the Juvenile Detention Center. Oh yeah Tutu, by the way, your boy Tree ain't loyal, just so you know."

"Man, I mean Detective, gone with that. My boy loyal. He been A1 since day one."

"Yeah?" Barrows said with a wicked grin. "Let's put that theory to the test. I'm gone show you something."

The detective ushered him into the room on the other side of the two-way mirror. Tutu saw Tree sitting across the table from Detective Millsap. Barrows flipped on the intercom switch on the wall beside the mirror so they could hear what was being said in the room.

"...you trying to go to jail?" Detective Millsap asked. "We already know you did it."

"Why is you keep saying that?" Tree whined. "I already told you a hundred times it was Tutu that was shooting. Do one of those gunpowder tests on his hands. I ain't lying. He always be shooting at people since he got shot up. Ask anybody from our hood."

"So would you sign a statement saying that if you

had to?"

"Yes!" Tree affirmed.

"Would you take the stand?"

"Absolutely," Tree said. "I ain't finta be going to jail for no fake wannabe gangster rapper because he clout chasing. Y'all got me messed up."

As he watched as his friend betrayed him without any qualms, all Tutu could say was, "Wwwoooowwwww."

Barrows asked, "You heard enough?"

"More than enough. Take me out of here."

Detective Barrows led him to the squad room to start his paperwork. At his desk, Barrows undid the handcuffs from behind Tutu's back, leaving one on his wrist. The empty cuff he attached to the heavy wooden chair next to his desk and Tutu sat down. Barrows seated himself at the desk and typed in the password to his computer. He began to ask Tutu questions as he filled out the report.

Tutu answered the questions, but all the while his mind was on the $3,500 he wouldn't be getting because he would miss tonight's show. That fact made his pockets hurt, but it made his heart hurt to know he'd just witnessed his friend snitch on him, as easy as if he was ordering six wings with lemon pepper.

CHAPTER 13

Tutu walked into the gym at the Juvenile Detention Center with Pooh, and several other boys. They all had on navy crewneck sweatshirts with JTDC screen printed across them and khaki pants. They walked over and took a seat on the bleachers next to the court.

"We got next!" Pooh yelled to the boys on the court.

A boy sitting further down on the bleachers, said, "I already got next, some of y'all can run with me though because I ain't got em all."

"Nall homie, we got next," Pooh said aggressively.

"Simmer down bro," Tutu said. "Boy, I'm trying to go to the crib, I don't want no smoke. You ready to send it up over a basketball game." To the boy further down the bleachers, he said, "Aye bro, its good. A couple of us will run with you."

The boy nodded his head in agreement.

"Aye Tutu, you getting soft, you been in here too long," Pooh said.

"Boy gone head on. I'm on my way home and you think I'm finta jag that for nothing. I ain't slow."

"Well, I don't care," their associate named Tray D stated. "I ain't letting nobody get away with a damn thing. I don't care how petty it is, I'm standing on they necks."

Tutu chuckled. "Well bro, if this was six, seven months ago, I was with it, but now I'm like wait til I go home if you feelin' like that. If don't nobody disrespect me or put they hands on me or the guys, I don't want the smoke. I'm trying to see my mama and my girl, on God. Forget all that, Pooh finish telling me what Vah said happened with Tree snitch ass."

"Right. Check it. Vah said ain't nobody really been rocking with Tree since they got word about what happened with you. Vah say he bumped into buddy at this chick party in the 90s and he was acting weird. Vah say he slid on buddy, like what's up with it foolie. He say Tree was acting like he wanted to turn up, talking about he ain't rockin with Gray Street no more. Tree say he with Money Makin Marquette now. Vah told him cool because GSG ain't rocking with no snitches no way. He say buddy got heated on that one, said Tree acted like he wanted to pull it, but him, Danno, Con and a couple more of them had big poles on them."

Tutu shook his head. "That's crazy! Tree ass tweaking. Now he a Triple M??? That's cool though, because he a rat anyway. GSG don't need no disloyal goofies like that no way. I seen and heard that man snitch with my own eyes and ears. He ain't get charged with nothing and I'm in here. Now who the trick? We gone see when I get out."

Over by the gym room door, a staff member entered the gym and spoke to one of the staff members posted there. The staff member left his post and walked over to Tutu and his friends in the bleachers.

He said, "Tureon, let's go. They want you in the counselor's office. Kindle wanna see you."

"Man we bout to hoop. We got next, gimme a minute," Tutu responded.

"Now man, let's go! Now!" the staff member ordered as he pointed toward the gym room door. "Right now, little hard head boy!"

"Man, Kindle don't even really want nothing," Tutu grumbled as he got up. "Somebody take my spot. When I come back I want my spot back though. And y'all bet not lose."

Tutu pulled his pants up as he followed behind the staff member.

∎∎∎

Tutu sat outside of his counselor, Lawrence Kindle's, office waiting to be seen. He could see through the office window that Kindle, as he was known in the Detention Center. was talking to another boy. Tutu thumbed through a Sports Illustrated as he waited. He wasn't really mad about coming to the counselor's office; he actually liked Kindle.

Kindle was as a huge, bearded Black man, with dreadlocks that hung to the middle of his back. He was as cool as they came, but he wasn't soft. He was once on his way to becoming a star basketball player, but he tore his Achilles tendon in a game while in college. A friend of his mother's that worked for Cook County got him this job and he'd been there for 17 years. He always kept it real with all the boys and girl inmates he came in contact with during his counseling sessions. He was notorious for never sugarcoating things. He could be quoted for always telling them he wasn't their babysitter or parent, so he didn't have to tell them what they wanted to hear. As he waited, Tutu looked at the pictures in the magazine he was holding, but he was much too distracted to read much of any of the articles. He was thinking about his future, something that had kept him up for the last few nights, now that he was close to being released.When he first got locked up, it felt like he was the next rapper to blow up coming out of Chicago. He had a hot video doing numbers on Youtube.com and his single had been finding its way onto Chicago radio stations. Geno told him that show offers were rolling in, but the moment promoters found out that he was locked up, the offers dried up quickly.

In the beginning he thought that once he was released it wouldn't have been too hard to remind the streets how lit he was on the rap side, because it wasn't like he'd been away for years. It was only seven months. To complicate matters though, the feds had snatched Geno and seized many of his assets, including the studio. Geno had violated quite a few federal drug laws and they had taken him into custody. His arrest and their seizure of the studio meant that Savage Life Records was over before it started.

As a result of Geno's arrest, Pekoe packed up and moved to Atlanta to do music with a cousin of his from down there. As for Freethrow, a few of his beats ended up getting heard by the right ears of some record label execs. They immediately wrote him some huge checks to produce several projects. He was currently in California barricaded in a studio and he wasn't accepting anyone's phone calls from back home in Chicago.

While he was in there, his friend Air had gotten shot in the back and was now confined to a wheelchair because he was paralyzed from the waist down. Pooh was in there with him because he tried to carjack an off-duty policeman when he needed a ride home. His friend Con, who was usually the mild one of the bunch was said to have killed at least three people. Someone from Payback City, a neighborhood they'd never had beef with before, decided to rob Con's grandmother and shot her in the arm when she wouldn't give up her cell phone. Con had gotten hold of a Glock and had been wilding out ever since.

Vah was still Vah though. Pooh said he had fallen in love with popping pills like X, Molly, and Mids. He was always rolling off hittas, as he called them. Pooh said he made sure he stayed as high as possible at all times. In his absence, Danno and Price had taken advantage of an out of town plug Geno had given them, so they had an unlimited connection for exotic weed and pills.

Everyone had changed Tutu realized, even him. In the months since he'd been here, he managed to pack on some muscle thanks to gambling at cards and dice for pushups. He began to like the changes he was seeing in his arms and chest, so he began to work out more and play sports on a regular basis. He always went to the alternative school in the Detention Center, though it was mandatory, he found that he actually liked some of the classes.

The hardest part of being locked up, besides being away from home and not being free, was the visits for him. Visits from loved ones were supposed to make you feel good, and he knew there were many inmates that didn't get any visits and would have loved to receive one, but for him they were torture. Whether it was Meeka, Neeka or his girlfriend Misha, he hated the range of emotions he went through on visiting day. He went from anticipation to joy to depressive sadness when his visitors would come and go, and all in a matter of hours. He found it much easier to write letters, and though Meeka wouldn't write him much, his auntie Neeka and Misha wrote him regularly.

Ever since Misha had started visiting him in the hospital when he'd gotten shot, they had been keeping in touch with one another. Before he'd been arrested they had started getting closer, but while he was in here, she had become his lifeline once she promised to be his girlfriend. Just the thought of her beautiful face, infectious laugh and shapely figure chased away his blues on many a day. He would read and reread her letters often, and replay the highlights of their telephone conversations in his head to help with the loneliness. He couldn't wait to get out and see her.

He looked up from the magazine and into Kindle's office. Kindle was through talking to the kid that was in his office because the boy got up and left. The counselor pulled a file folder in front of him, looked up at Tutu and beckoned to him through the glass. He got up and brushed past the exiting boy to go inside the office. He took a seat in the chair in front of Kindle's desk.

"What up old head," Tutu said by way of greeting.

"The name is Kindle or your Majesty, pick one," Kindle growled.

"Okay, Kindle. What's up with it though?"

"This young sir is your exit interview, Mr. Young," Kindle announced as he opened the file in front of him."

Tutu leaned forward in his chair. "Okay, that's what I like to hear. Exit interview. I like the sound of that."

Kindle laughed. "Alright, young buck, when I first started doing this some years ago, I used to have this long ass speech I would give. Realized it was a waste of breath and stopped doing it. I'm looking at your file. While you were here you didn't do too, too bad. There's some gang activity here I see, but on the other hand you didn't do too bad in school. Couple of fights, never been caught with contraband. You're not the best of the best or the worst of worst." Kindle closed his file and looked him in his eyes. "Best thing I can do is give it you straight, young buck. If you go out there and do the same thing, you gone get the same results. Period."

"That's it?" Tutu asked.

"Yup. That's it. There's no real secret to staying out of here. Just don't do the stuff that will get you in here. That works for the most part. Riding and sliding in the streets, hanging and banging is gone land you in places like this or in the ground. Simple as that. If you do what you've always done, you're going to get what you've always got. Any questions?"

Though the look on Tutu's face said that he had a million questions, he remained silent. He shook his head and said, "Nope Kindle, I ain't got no questions. I'm good. I just wanna get out of here and go to the crib."

Kindle took one of his business cards from the card holder on his desk. He used his pen to write a number on the back of the card and handed it to Tutu.

"Look young buck, those are my numbers, my office and cell. I mentor and counsel outside of here, so you can hit me up if you in a jam that I may be able to help you out of. Now you need to know, I don't loan money so don't ask. I'm not going to rent you a car or co-sign a loan for you, and I can't get you in no strip clubs."

"That's wassup, my man Kindle making it rain in the strip clubs." he said with a laugh.

"Boy on my salary, I can't even make it drizzle. It's gone be clear skies," Kindle quipped. "Get yo mind out the gutter, boy. I'm putting together a teen basketball league that will play at Chicago State University, so I wanna hear from you, that'll give you something to do with your time. Other than that, good luck young brother, I hope everything works out for you. Now get out of here."

He stood up and saluted Kindle. "Aw-ight, Kindle. I'ma walk light out there. I'll see you in the world."

Kindle reached out his hand to shake Tutu's. "I hope so, little brother, I really hope so." Tutu strode out of Kindle's office and the staff member that delivered him there fell into step with him as he walked back to the gym for one of the last few times.

CHAPTER 14

Tutu put two pieces of pizza onto his plate and closed the pizza box. He sat back on the couch with his paper plate. Misha looked quite comfortable wearing leggings and one of his t-shirts, as she was searching the Netflix menu on the living room television, looking for something to watch. Her feet were swept up under her on the couch. She picked the movie Shottas and put the remote on the coffee table.

Tutu dumped Parmesan cheese on his pizza slices. He said, "Bae, you want some more of this pizza?"

"I'm full, Tutu, I can't eat another piece. I done already ate too much. I think you trying to get me fat."

"Like you needed any help with that," he quipped, as he gave her little belly a side eye glance. "You already doing pretty good on your own."

"Shut up, boy," she said playfully as she punched him on his arm. He fixed a serious look on his face, but he could barely contain his smile.

"Stop it girl, you see the movie on. Gone now."

"I ain't trying to hear that," Misha said. She scooted closer to him and tickled him.

They played around for a few moments, before they settled down to watch the movie. Tutu finished eating his pizza slices and put the plate on the table. He wiped his hands and mouth with a napkin and tossed it on his plate. He sat back and put his arm around her shoulders. She snuggled closer and they remained that way until the movie went off. When it was over, Tutu sat forward and stretched.

"Wanna watch another one, girl?" he asked.

Misha replied, "I guess, but more than likely it's gone be watching me."

Tutu used the remote control to begin scrolling through the Netflix selections when his cell phone rang. Misha looked at the phone and then looked at him.

"Who is that?" she inquired.

"Dag, you thirsty, I don't know." Tutu picked up his phone and looked at the caller I.D.; it was his aunt Neeka. To Misha, he said, "Oh yeah, this my heart right here. One of my favorite girls. She musta felt how much I was missing her."

Before he could answer the phone, Misha snatched it. She looked at the caller I.D. and saw it was his aunt. "Stop playing with me, boy," she said as she handed the phone back to him.

With a smile on his face, Tutu answered the call. "Hey Auntie, how's my mama's twin?"

Misha slapped him in the back of his head. He held his hand off the phone mic and mouthed, "On God, stop playing, you see my Auntie on the phone."

He switched the phone to the speaker mode as he looked at his girlfriend. "My bad, I dropped my phone. Now what was you saying Auntie?"

"Yeah Tutu, I was just calling to check up on you. Meeka told me you be staying in the house. What's going on?"

"Just trying to stay out the way Auntie. It's a lot of snake ish going on out here. I'm in the crib watching Netflix, I'm not on anything. I don't want no smoke and the way these big mouth lames be tricking I ain't trying to get locked back up."

"I know that's right Tutu," his aunt agreed. "You gotta make yo next move your best move though."

"I know right. How Que doing away at school though?"

"He good, he just miss that little ugly girlfriend of his. Whole campus full of women and he miss her big teeth butt. He wished she woulda went down there to school with him, but I'm glad she didn't. He don't have too much time to sit around though, with football season about to start. I told him he better get in that weight room and quit worrying about that bug."

Tutu laughed. "Nall, your son EJ is the bug." It was Neeka's turn to laugh. "I didn't say that he wasn't." They both laughed for a bit, then Neeka's tone sobered up. "So what you gone do, nephew?"

"About what?"

"About school? About a job? You just can't sit around the house all day waiting on my twin to give you some money so you can smoke."

"I don't even smoke no more, Auntie," Tutu announced proudly, though he didn't admit that now he smoked cigarettes.

"You don't smoke weed?" Neeka asked, with a tone of disbelief.

"For real, for real. And I'm going to get my G.E.D. too. All I gotta do is go take the test."

"Nephew, if you don't smoke weed, I coulda been

got you a job. You know I manage the Home Depot on Western. Don't you want a job? The pay is not bad."

Neeka could hear the hesitation in his voice when, he said, "I on't know about that one T.T., I got enemies. The opps would love…"

"Boy! Ain't none of yo doggone opps gone be at Home Depot on Western Avenue. You making that up. If you really is trying to stay out the way, a job is the best thing for you."

Tutu looked over at Misha and she was nodding her head in total agreement. "She ain't lying," Misha mouthed.

"Hold on for one sec, Auntie," Tutu said as he looked at Misha. He switched off the speakerphone mode and held his cell phone to his ear. "Auntie, I ain't never had no job before, I don't know about that life."

"Well, ain't no better time than the present," Neeka answered. "My twin ain't finta be taking care of yo overgrown butt forever. Yeah, you gone do this. Get yo resume together, if you ain't got one, make one up. I'm gone drop off a application for you, you gone fill it out, and that's that. Now, I gotta go. Love you, nephew."

"Love you too, Auntie," Tutu grumbled, before ending the call. He looked over at Misha. "Not one word from you. Not one."

Misha made a motion like she was locking her lips and throwing away the key. They sat there in silence pretending to watch the next movie.

Finally, without looking at her, Tutu asked, "What you gotta say, girl?"

"I agree with your Auntie," Misha gushed as if the floodgates were opened. "What's wrong with getting a job and finishing school? You gotta think about your future. It's time. You almost died Tutu, but God gave you a second chance. Don't you want to do something with that chance? You obviously as sick of these streets as I am. I know because you didn't run straight back to them when you got out. I know I'm tired of all this shooting and killing. My friend Mimi is dead, and you could have been too. I think it's time to do something else is all I'm saying. Ain't nothing out here for you."

"You act like I'm out here drilling. I ain't on no savage stuff. I'm trying to do the music thing. You seen what I can do. We can be rich, bae. You going to school for business too. That way when I get this bread for us, you can invest it and flip it like crazy."

Misha brought her knees up and wrapped her arms around them. "Tutu, you gotta know the rap thing is a real long shot. I believe in you bae, but what if you don't make it?"

"I got bars though," he protested. "You heard me. You know what I can do. These other rappers out here don't want it with me."

Misha rolled her eyes. "You know that don't mean nothing. It's rappers out here that's straight trash and they get on, while dudes that can really rap ain't going nowhere. You need more than rap skills is what I'm saying."

"Well how am I gone ever know if I coulda made it if I'm stuck in a orange apron, helping dudes find nails at Home Depot?"

Misha got on her knees and put her arms around his neck. "Look bae, I'm not saying don't do your music. All I'm saying is if you work, you can stack you some bread, and put your own music out. It may take you a little longer, but you'll own your stuff. All I'm saying is you should try. And one more thing."

"What's that?"

"It sounds like Aunt Neeka not going no way. She not taking no for an answer."

He sighed and rolled his eyes because he didn't want to tell Misha she was right. His text message alert chirped on his cell phone. He picked it up and opened the message.

Vah: gang wyo

Tutu: no thing!

Vah: u @ the crib

Tutu: yea

Vah: finna slide

Tutu: come on

He stood and took a cigarette from his pack on the table. He announced, "Vah finta fall through. I'm on the porch."

Misha stretched her long legs out on the couch. "Well, I'm about to take a nap."

On the front porch, Tutu took a seat on an orange milk crate. He lit his cigarette and looked up and down the block. As he looked at his surroundings, it never ceased to amaze him how much the block had changed in the last six or seven years. His street used to be full of homes and two flat buildings. Children would play on the sidewalks and in yards, and people would pick up trash. Cars used to line both sides of the streets, and neighbors would speak and help one another out.

In those days, all of his friends lived either on his Gray Street block or the next one. He couldn't remember exactly when the violence started to escalate here and in the surrounding neighborhoods. It just seemed like one day they were playing ball in the street, and the next day somebody was doing a drive-by shooting on the same block. From that day forward it got worse and worse.

People started moving out to get away from the violence. Former Chicago Housing Authority dwellers started moving on the blocks, courtesy of the City tearing down the projects, and giving them Section 8. A couple of homes burnt down and some were abandoned. Suddenly people stopped acting neighborly. There were no more block parties, block cleaning days, or back-to-school fun days. The cars began to disappear as the people moved out. Fast forward to today, and Tutu was actually the last of his friends living on the same street; the same street where his brother was murdered. The crazy thing was there were now more people than ever killing and dying in the name of the Gray Street Gang, but they didn't live there.

Down the block, Tutu noticed Vah across the street coming in his direction. He could see that Vah was talking to himself, complete with hand movements and swinging at imaginary insects. Several times he stopped to examine objects on the ground before continuing on. Though he hadn't wanted to at first, he had to admit his childhood homie wasn't right no more. Supposedly he had popped some bad Molly and it had done something to his brain. His hair was now a matted, tangled mess and he was rarely clean these days. He tended to speak in choppy sentences about several different subjects at a time, making it hard to follow his conversation. He walked up and sat on the same spot on Tutu's porch he'd been sitting in for years without speaking.

"Gang nem, waddup," Tutu said by way of greeting.

"I don't know what's up and I'm trying to get to the bottom of that, you feel me," answered Vah.

"What you on, bro?"

"I ain't on anything Tutu. I just wanted to see one of the homies that ain't never switched up on me. I miss you and Tyrese and the guys. Things changed. On God, I miss my granny. On Gray Street, her chicken was better than Popeye's chicken…"

For a while Tutu listened to Vah's confusing conversation. He took another cigarette from his pack and lit it with the cigarette butt he was smoking already before tossing it away. When he couldn't take any more of Vah's rambling, he asked, "Damn, gang, what happened to you?"

Vah stopped babbling and thought about it for a moment. He said, "Bro, I was just trying to party and feel good. Somebody gave me a hitter at a party I was at, I took it, and I feel like I can't come down no more. I ain't had no Molly, or X in some weeks now, but I still want a good gyro. I ain't had a good gyro since King Subs burnt down."

He paused and hit his forehead several times with the palm of his hand like he was trying to jumpstart his brain. "That's what I'm talking about bro. On God, it gets real hard to keep my thoughts from being mixed up. Tutu, I forget stuff and remember everything all at once. Sometimes I get so sad thinking about things, I wanna cry, but then I forget why I wanna cry in the first place. I'm thinking about going to Miami with gang and them. Show them ATL boys they don't know nothing about Chiraq savages. How you been though bro?"

Tutu shrugged. "I'm good I guess. Right now I'm just trying to stay out the way and see what I wanna do with myself. I want to get back into the music, but my auntie and my OG is trying to finesse me into getting a job."

"You said that like it's a bad thing bro," Vah said as he rocked back and forth. "I wish I could work and get away from this madness every day, but I'm a Gray Street G 'til I die. 8 Deuce Killer, on gang. You though, Tutu, I suggest you don't get peanut butter on yo shoes, because when it rain you should go in the house."

"I feel you Vah, but I feel like everybody gone be trying to say I'm soft, if I ain't out here putting pressure on these lames about my brother and gang."

"You already done put in work Tutu. Savage ain't gang no more. You feel me? They like ice cream sandwiches out here. I mean pancakes. Forget what they talking about bro. On God, get you a job and do the school thing. Ain't nothing wrong with that. I wish I woulda stayed in school, you feel. Is you cold?"

Before Tutu could answer, Vah got up and jumped down the porch steps. He stumbled a bit on the landing, but managed to keep his footing.

"Where you going, bro?" Tutu asked.

"I really don't know, but I gotta keep moving," Vah called out over his shoulder. He stopped a few feet away and looked back at Tutu. "Step on a crack, break yo mama's back bro. I love you, gang. You'll always be one of mines even if you got a job or you graduate."

"Love you too, bro," Tutu replied. "My A1 since day one." He stood up and watched Vah walk away, taking care not to step on any cracks in the sidewalk. He knew his friend was playing Step On A Crack, Break Yo Mama's Back, a game they'd played since they were shorties. He flicked the cigarette butt over into the gangway and went back inside the apartment. Misha wasn't on the couch where he'd left her.

"Misha! Misha!" he yelled.

Further down the hallway, the bathroom door opened and Misha came out of it, drying her hands on a paper towel.

"Boy, what you want? Why you in here calling my name like you done lost your mind?"

"Will you make me a resume?" Tureon asked sheepishly. "And help me fill out this application when my T.T. bring it?"

Misha flashed a 100 watt smile. "Of course I will bae."

CHAPTER 15

Tutu sat at a lunch table in the break room of the Home Depot where he worked with three of his fellow co-workers. They all wore orange aprons with the Home Depot logo silk screened on them, as they argued about the upcoming Chicago Bears season opener. The argument had ensued because Tutu's co-worker named Gary was a Green Packers fan, their opponent for the upcoming game, and division rivals.

"I thought you were real cool until now, Gary," said their co-worker named Charlotte. "I would have never took you for a cheesehead. Tureon this yo boy too."

"Yeah, I ain't mad at him, if he rolling with Rodgers he a smart man," Tutu said, giving Gary a high five. "I don't see what the problem is."

"Not you too," said his co-worker named Larry. "You gotta be kidding me. Why am I not surprised? I wouldn't even be mad if y'all was Tom Brady, I mean Patriots fans."

"Y'all tweaking," added their co-worker named Akeem.

"Y'all two must have never heard of the '85 Bears."

"Really? You really saying that?" Tureon asked. "Man, the Bears been losing my entire life bro. My entire life!

And y'all still talking about them."

"On my baby," Gary agreed. "They ain't won since Mike Ditka was the coach."

"Excuse me, but somehow you seem to have forgotten about Lovie Smith, the greatest Bears coach ever," pointed out Charlotte. "He coached Urlacher, the third best linebacker in Bears history, after Mike Singletary and Wilbur Marshall."

"Aww, here we go," said Tutu as tossed his hands up in the air. "Next they gone tell us we should sacrifice our first born sons to Walter Payton. Gone head with that."

"Every time they win two pre-season games, they think they going to the Superbowl," Gary added. "Bears fans be irrational as hell."

"I'm saying," Tutu agreed. "They about to be one and 15 this season again."

"I bet our season record is gone be better than the Packers," challenged Akeem. "I bet a deep dish pizza on it and you gotta go get it in that new car of yours."

"Bet, Akeem," Tutu said, as he offered his hand to shake. "My car ain't new though."

"It's new to you ain't it?" Gary asked.

He nodded. "Then it's new," they all chimed in with a laugh.

Tutu couldn't help but grin. He liked his co-workers. Most of them were friendly and helpful, and they acted like a huge family. Their lunch break was coming to an end, so they took their last bites and sips, and began to clean up their table. Tutu ate the last few chips left in his bag and swooped up his mess. He gulped the remainder of his raspberry iced tea and threw away his garbage.

"I'm out of here," Tutu announced. "I'm not trying to be late getting back to the floor. I'm trying to get that Employee of the Month plaque and that bonus, and I'm not about to mess that up, by being late because of arguing with some Packer haters."

As they joked with one another on the way to the sales floor, Tutu thought how if he had to have a job, this one wasn't bad at all. It was actually laughable to him, that at first he had been afraid to work here. His aunt had been real easy to deal with and had walked him straight through the hiring process without a hitch. Her only demand was that he cut his dreads, which he had grown tired of any way.

From the first day, the people he worked with made him feel welcome, and they were patient as they trained him. After his third week on the job, he actually found himself looking forward to going to work. He even found that he liked helping customers and listening to the stories of the carpenters, plumbers and tradesmen. He'd made it past his 90 day probation over two months ago with ease. Once he saw what his checks would look like with overtime, he would get there early and leave late whenever possible. Also he wouldn't tell them, but he liked how proud his mother Meeka, his aunt Neeka and his girlfriend Misha were of him. He knew his mom and auntie had pretty much written him off as a savage, but it felt good for them to look at him like he had a chance now.

In the past few months, he'd been able to stack a few bands and managed to buy himself a reasonably clean 2008 Grand Prix, from one of his cousin Que's friends for a good deal. In a couple of weeks, he got the hang of the driving thing and though he still didn't have his license, he was going to work on it. A vehicle had been a must for him because he wasn't going to ride the bus. In the beginning, his aunt Neeka would pick him up and drop him off, and he would Uber to work on days she wasn't going into the store. He'd been so worried about bumping into some of his enemies here, but in close to six months he hadn't seen any of his opps.

Before they went to their department, Akeem detoured to the restroom.

"See you on the floor, Tureon. Gotta pay my water bill real quick."

"Alright, 'Keem," he said, as he went to clock back in from lunch.

The moment he walked back out onto the store floor, he barely had time to tie his apron on when the customers started coming in droves. He didn't even get a chance to take a smoke break it got so busy. Next thing he knew it was quitting time. Before he went to clock out, his section supervisor asked if he wanted to close, and to his surprise, Tutu actually said no. As he headed for the locker room, he thought about how much he hated missing those sweet overtime hours, but he had plans with Misha later. In one of her classes, she was pitching a business plan she'd wrote to real investors. She wanted him to be at the presentation for good luck and she wasn't taking no for an answer.

As it was, he would have just enough time to shower, change clothes and get to her school without a moment to spare. The minute his shift was over, he punched out and raced for the employee locker room. He tossed his apron in his locker, grabbed his hoodie and book bag, and left the locker room. In the parking lot, he started his car and pulled from the parking space, narrowly missing two men pushing a cart full of drywall sheets. He held up his hand in apology and maneuvered around them.

In less than 20 minutes he was putting his key in the front door of his mother's apartment on Gray Street. He kicked his work boots off at the door and dashed to his bedroom. In his room, he threw up the GSG sign to the cardboard cutout of his brother Tyrese. He'd had it made for Tyrese's birthday a month ago. Quickly he got undressed, grabbed his underwear and went to take a shower. He took one of the quickest showers of his life, and soon he was dressed. After a couple of sprays of cologne, he slipped his feet into a new pair of Mikes and checked his reflection in the mirror. Satisfied he headed for the door.

"Aw-ight Tyrese, love you boy," he said to his brother's cut-out.

He left the apartment and was pulling into the Chicago State University parking lot in 15 minutes. He parked and jogged to the building where Misha was making her presentation. In the building, he slipped into the large lecture hall and scanned the room to locate Misha. She was sitting at a table in front of the room with four other applicants. What had to be the investors were sitting in the first and second rows, currently listening to a girl from India nervously present her business plan.

He took a seat in the back of the room, and tried to understand the presentation, but the girl was too nervous, making her already heavy accent almost impossible to understand. The next presenter cracked too many corny jokes and Tutu could tell the investors were unimpressed, some even appeared to be annoyed. Misha was next after the corny dude and the intelligent, confident, professional way she delivered her presentation floored everyone, including him. He knew she seemed to know what she was talking about when it came to business, but now he saw firsthand that she really knew a lot about it. He actually noticed some of the investors sit up and hang on her every word.

Two more students presented their plans after Misha, and then the investors had a question and answer session for the candidates. They largely focused on Misha almost totally ignoring the other candidates. His chest swelled with pride as he watched his girlfriend in her glory; her skin seemed to be glowing as she made her points. Many of the investors were nodding favorably at her facts and figures. Finally they all seemed to be satisfied and the head of the business school announced the presentation part was over. Immediately following there was a reception for the guests while the investors made their decisions.

The guests all filed out of the room to the lobby where the reception was being held. He was standing off to the side enjoying a shrimp cocktail when Misha came rushing over. She had the biggest smile on her face as she gave him a spine crushing hug.

"They're going to fund my project!" she gushed. "Bae, they were fighting over me and ended up teaming up. They're tripling what I asked for. We about to be balling!"

Tutu laughed as he hugged her. "You did your thing up there, ma. They better have put they bread on you, the rest of them was lames anyway. I'm proud of you,

Misha. I barely heard a word you was saying though, you was looking so thick and pretty up there."

Misha hit him softly on the chest. "How proud was you?"

"So proud that dinner is on me."

Misha smiled. "Good, because I wasn't trying to fill up on veggie plates and cheese. I gotta make my rounds, shake hands and smile, thank a few people and then we can get low. Take my laptop for me."

"What you got a taste for?" Tutu asked as he removed her computer case from her shoulder.

Misha screwed up her face in thought for a moment, then snapped her fingers. "Pizza. Nall, nall. Tacos. Nall scratch that. You paying, I want some seafood."

"Aww, here you go," he said, rolling his eyes to the ceiling.

"Yup, I want a crab leg and shrimp boil from that restaurant right there on 87th Street before you get to Stony Island. And don't be acting like that because you shole be eating it right along with me."

Tutu grinned. He said, "Gone head on girl before the only shrimp you be eating is the ones on that table over there. You better get over there now because that big chick right there just noticed them. If you want, I can put a few in my pocket for you."

"You ain't even funny boy," Misha said as she walked away. "What you is, is petty. Now just hold that bag 'til I get back."

In her absence, Tutu snacked on different cheeses and tried a few of the fancier items on the refreshment table. Most of those ended up balled up in a napkin after he spit them back out. From across the room he watched Misha shake hands and talk with the school staff and the few investors that hung around for the reception. After a bit, she detached herself from an especially creepy looking investor and made her way to him.

As she walked past Tutu toward the exit, she stage whispered from the side of her mouth, "Come on boy, I just told them I was going to bathroom, but we out. Now bring yo slow walking self on."

Misha's heels clicked loudly on the tile of the empty hallway as they made their way out of the business school building. Outside in the car, she kicked off her shoes and untucked her blouse. Tutu drove the car from the parking lot and off the campus.

Misha reached over and turned down the radio, causing him to glance over at her. "I can taste them crab legs now," she said. "I could eat crab legs, shrimp, and lobster every day for breakfast, lunch and dinner."

"Yeah, I know. That's all you be wanting to eat. I want me a steak or pork chops or something. Some soul food."

Misha made a face and rubbed her stomach. "Just the smell of meat be turning my stomach nowadays. It's like I can smell the blood in it or something. It be making me want to throw up. And I definitely don't want no pork in my body. The other day this lady was eating a big ole double cheeseburger in the café next to me and I almost threw up. Sometimes the smell of coffee can do that too."

"Yeah and don't let me light a square, you act like I'm smoking crack. I can't even smoke in my own car or crib."

"Don't nobody want to get cancer from you and Meeka's secondhand smoke. Right now though, don't none of that matter, I can't wait to get somewhere so I can take off this skirt. The cleaners must have shrunk my clothes, because this skirt didn't even used to be tight. You should have seen me trying to wiggle into it."

Tutu glanced over at her. He said, "I ain't wanna say nothing, I knew you was looking thick. I just thought it was all the butter you eating with all these crab legs."

Misha looked down at her stomach and rubbed it again. "I have put on a couple of pounds. Just stress eating trying to get through this presentation. I'll start back working out next week."

"Just don't get rid of that booty," he warned. "I like that."

"Shut up boy," she said, as she used the power lever to make her seat recline. "I need to close my eyes for a minute. I couldn't sleep all night making last minute changes. Wake me up when you get the food."

He let her doze as he drove to the restaurant on 87th Street. He drove into the strip mall parking lot and found a space to back into in front of the place.

"Make sure you get me a ginger ale," Misha murmured as she turned on her side.

Without answering, he left the car and went inside to order their food.

In an older model black Chevy Impala sitting at the stoplight on 87th Street, Donnie tapped Shannon on the shoulder. Shannon was driving and Donnie was riding in the front passenger seat.

"That's Tutu going in that restaurant," Donnie said excitedly.

"Where?" Shannon asked. Donnie pointed across Shannon's face. "Right there! No right there boy!"

Shannon drove slowly through the intersection when the light changed to green; he spotted Tutu. "That is ole wanna be tough ass Tutu. I ain't seen him in a minute. Where he been?"

"Don't none of that even make no difference, we on his heels," said Donnie. "He can't live. I want my lick back, them goofies tried to clout up off me. I can't go."

"I'ma spin the block," Shannon said. He looked over his shoulder at the boy in the back seat of his car. "Shoota, you ready?"

In the backseat, a skinny young boy no older than 15 sat gripping a 30-shot Glock. His eyes were huge and his lips were twisted from the effects of the pill he'd just taken a while ago. Instead of answering, Shoota pulled the hood of his sweatshirt over his dreadlocks and jacked a round into the chamber of his gun.

"Look boy, don't be scared, Tutu a goofy, he ain't got no banger on him," Donnie said. "Soon as we pull up on them, you air the car out. You hear me?"

"Yeah," Shoota said. "Slide, I got it."

After circling the block, Shannon parked on the side street across from the strip mall. As they waited for Tutu to come out of the restaurant, Shoota fidgeted with the gun in the back seat. Fifteen minutes later, Tutu came out of the restaurant across the street. He was carrying an aluminum pan of seafood and a plastic bag with several pops in it. He walked around to the passenger side of the car to give the food to Misha. He knew she would want to snack on the shrimp and broccoli as they rode to his apartment.

He sat the pan on the roof of the car and fished his keys out of his pocket. Using the alarm button he unlocked the car and opened the front passenger door. Misha opened her eyes when the door opened and stretched like a cat.

"Here you go with yo greedy butt," he said with a smile.

A huge smile lit up her face as she reached out for the pan with both of her hands. Simultaneously, a black Impala sped into the parking lot and screeched to a stop behind Tutu's car. The pan was still in his hands as he looked over at the car and directly into Donnie's face. Tutu saw Shoota raise up in the backseat and point his gun out the window, and began to pull the trigger.

A split second before the first shot rang out, Tutu dropped the food and dove past his open car door to the ground. Once there, he rolled to the right under a Dodge Caravan parked next to his car. Gunshots went off for what seemed like forever to Tutu as he lay beneath the minivan. The shots stopped and he heard the screech of tires as the Impala peeled away.

He waited for a few moments and then cautiously slid from under the van. His assailants were gone so he ran around the van to his car. As he went to get in the car he looked at the shattered glass windows of the restaurant. Inside, he saw an elderly lady kneeling on the floor beside her husband. She was crying as she held his lifeless hand. His open eyes were fixed on the restaurant's menu board on the wall.

His hands were shaking as he started the car. For the first time he noticed there were bullet holes in the windshield, several on the passenger side. He put the car in gear and saw that Misha's door was still open. "Close the door, Misha, we gotta go."

When Misha didn't respond he looked over at her.

Her head was resting against the doorjamb and he could see blood on her blouse; a lot of blood.

"Misha! Misha!" he yelled in horror. "Baby! Baby, wake up and close the door! Stop playing girl!"

Still nothing.

He shook her shoulder softly as he sobbed.

"Misha baby, please wake up. I need you to close the door baby, please."

She didn't move or answer.

"I'll get it for you. Hold on baby, I'm gone get you to the hospital and get you some help. Just hold on."

Tutu's car rocketed out of the parking lot, and cut off a Hyundai as he swung into traffic. He raced to Stony Island and almost flipped the car as he made a left turn. He righted the car and shot north on Stony, blowing his horn at drivers and running every red light he could on his way. Recklessly he swerved into the hospital's emergency room loading zone and braked sharply. He scrambled from the car and ran inside the sliding cars.

"Help me! Help me!" he shouted in the lobby. "Please, somebody help my girlfriend. She been shot. Help her!" His pleas spurred the emergency room staff into action.

"Where is she?" asked the security officer at the desk.

"She's outside in my car. She's not talking or moving."

The nurse came from behind the desk, and she said, "Show us."

As they ran for the doors, they were followed by two security guards, and another nurse. A nurses' assistant ran to get a gurney and followed them outdoors. Outside, several people had gathered and were looking at the car and peeking at Misha. Tutu ran over to the car, opened the passenger door and was trying to get Misha's seatbelt undone when the desk nurse took charge.

"You're going to have to move out of the way, sir," she said urgently. Sure handedly she unbuckled the seatbelt. "Where's that cart? I need it!"

The nurse's assistant burst through the emergency doors with the bed for transport and together they all lifted Misha from the car. When they lifted her to place her on the bed, Tutu could see her back was covered in blood. The emergency room staff hurriedly pushed her inside as he followed them. Inside the building, he tried to follow them through another pair of double doors into the emergency care treatment unit, but a security officer stopped him.

"You can't go back there man," the officer said. "You gone have to move that car out the lane. Park in the lot and come back in and register her."

Tutu was prepared to argue that it was more important he go with his girlfriend, but the officer stood in his path.

"Look little brother," he said gently. "I know you're worried, but let them do what they do. The best thing right now is for you to move the car and come get her registered. Just do that for us."

"Okay, okay," he replied. He ran back to his car and got in the driver's seat. He drove out of the emergency room lane and across the street to the parking lot. He looked over at the passenger seat, there was a pool of blood in it. He left the parked car and called Meeka with tears in his eyes as he walked back to the emergency room.

CHAPTER 16

In the emergency operation waiting room, Tutu sat on the edge of his seat between his mother Meeka and his aunt Neeka. His head was in his hands and tear tracks stained his face. Neeka's arm was around his shoulders, while Meeka rubbed his back. Across from them sat Misha's grandmother and her older brother Carmichael. The grandmother was shooting daggers with her eyes at Tutu and Neeka was rolling her eyes at the grandmother in return.

In the next two hours, friends and family of both Tutu and Misha joined them. Around the room, people were praying, talking quietly and trying to figure out what happened as they all waited for news about Misha's condition. At 10:17 on the dot, a scrub wearing doctor stepped in the room.

"Excuse me, I'm looking for the parents of Carmisha," the doctor announced, looking in Tutu, Neeka and Meeka's direction. "I have news about her condition."

Misha's grandmother, got to her feet with help from her grandson. "That ain't her mama, her mama passed on, my only daughter. You can tell me what you have to say, I'm responsible for her."

The doctor bluntly asked, "I'm unclear, are you her next of kin? Because she doesn't require a guardian."

Misha's grandmother was taken aback by the question and the doctor's tone, but she answered, "Well, I guess I am her next of kin, I'm her grandmother. And if that's not good enough, this is her brother."

"Would you like for me to give you an update here? Or in the hallway?" asked the doctor.

The grandmother looked around the room, making sure she fixed Tutu with a hateful glare. "No sir, that's not necessary to do here. This is not her family. We are her only family. We'll step out into the corridor. It's not everybody's business no way."

Without ceremony, the doctor about-faced and left the waiting room with Misha's grandmother and brother in his wake. Tutu looked at his mother and aunt with an unbelieving look on his face. Meeka shrugged, but Neeka looked concerned.

"Wwwooowwww," Tutu said as he shook his head. "She cappin! I don't know what she on."

Neeka patted his back. "Don't even worry about all that. The most important thing is making sure Misha gone be alright. This is so crazy. Didn't you tell me her friend died in a expressway shooting?"

"Yeah Auntie. Right there by 67th. Somebody aired the car out she was in and she ain't make it. I was still in the hospital when it happened. Misha was coming up there talking to me about it. She said she was hurt by it, but she said it was a reminder about having good karma. She never said what that meant though."

"Well what was you doing today boy?" Meeka asked. "I thought you was working and wasn't in them streets no more?"

"Really? Really Mama? I live with you, how you don't know that. I ain't been hanging or nothing. I go to work and come home. I been trying to stay out the way."

"Well obviously you ain't do a good enough job," Meeka remarked.

Before Tutu could reply, they heard a blood-curdling scream. Everyone jumped up and ran into the hallway. Outside the waiting room, Misha's grandmother was on the floor and her brother was trying to get her up. Her wig had rolled to the side and her eyeglasses were lopsided. Tutu rushed over to help Carmichael help her up. They pulled her to her feet and as soon as she was standing, she snatched her arm away from Tutu.

"You get your damn hands off of me boy!" she raged. "Haven't you done enough to my granddaughter?"

"What's wrong with you? What are you talking about, I haven't done anything."

She tried to slap Tutu, but Carmichael stopped her. Tears were streaming down his face. "Grandma, that's enough."

"What happened?" Neeka asked anxiously.

"Misha didn't make it," Carmichael sobbed. "He said they tried, she lost too much blood."

"And she was pregnant by this heathen!" added Misha's grandmother angrily. "I knew this dog would destroy my grandbaby's life. I knew it. This was Jesus' way of punishing her for taking up with the likes of him."

Tutu looked at Carmichael for confirmation. "What? Nooooo!"

Carmichael nodded miserably. "Yeah she was

pregnant. Didn't nobody know. Did you?"

"No, no, no, no, no, no, no, no," Tutu repeated in shock as he sank to his knees. "No, no, no, no, no, no, no, no." Meeka put her hand on his shoulder, while his aunt Neeka knelt on the floor next to him, pulling her nephew close as great sobs wracked his body.

CHAPTER 17

Tutu walked south on Lawson Street to the corner. Lawson was two streets east of Gray Street, but it had been a GSG stronghold for quite some time after several OG's moved over there a decade ago. There were a few small cliques on Lawson Street when GSG Tommie, his brothers Arnie and Louie moved there, but they quickly converted them all into Gray Street Gang.

At the corner of the block, Tutu took his time as he crossed the street diagonally disregarding the cars at two different stops signs. The moment he was out of the middle of the intersection, one of the drivers sped off after cursing at him. Tutu ignored their curses and kept walking to the middle of the next block, to the building he was looking for. The yard was full of unkempt grass, and a scooter and two mini-bikes leaned against the fence. Three boys sat on the dark porch of the two story building.

When Tutu walked up to the gate, one of the boys on the porch chanted, "Loud, loud, loud. Sawbucks of loud right here homie."

Another boy announced, "I got Percs and Xans, foolie."

Tutu opened the gate and walked into the yard. "Nall, I'm good. I'm looking for Danno."

"Who you?" one boy asked distrustfully.

When Tutu didn't answer, the boy pulled a pistol from under his hoodie. "I said who you, boy? Gang nem don't know you. You look like a opp. If you ain't shopping, you need to get from through here for you get knocked down."

Con stepped from the shadows of the hallway behind the boys on the porch. "Boy, shuddup before you get hurt. You gone get enough of woofin at people."

"How I'm woofin?" the boy asked, trying to save face. "I don't know homie. He ain't gang."

Con shoved past the boy on the porch and walked down the stairs over to Tutu. He shook the GSG handshake with him.

"Boy, I was GSG before you jumped off the porch." Tutu said, as he hugged Con. "Waddup with it, Con?"

"I'm good, what you on Tutu?"

"I need to holla at Danno. He over here?"

"Yeah, c'mon. He and a couple of the guys upstairs playing bones."

As Tutu followed Con up the stairs and onto the porch, he gave the youngster that threatened him one last glare. Once they were in the hallway and out of earshot of the boys on the porch, and walking up the stairs, Con said, "Bro, sorry to hear about what happened to your girl. My condolences."

"Thanks bro," Tutu mumbled.

They continued up the stairs in silence. At the apartment door on the second floor, Con knocked three times, paused, and knocked twice more. An eye appeared at the peephole and next they heard the sound of several locks being unlocked. The apartment door swung open and Pooh stood there with a wide grin on his face.

"Aye yall, look who fell through the traphouse, Tutu from Gray Street," Pooh declared.

"Waddup gang."

With a sickly smile on his face, Tutu shook hands with Pooh. He and Con stepped inside the apartment.

"Waddup with it y'all," Tutu said.

Danno jumped to his feet almost knocking over the card table where Price and a boy Tutu didn't know had been playing dominoes. He rushed over to Tutu, showed him some love and gave him a huge hug. Price walked over much calmer and waited for his turn to show his homie some love. When Danno finally let him go, Price shook hands with him too, and gave him a hug.

"I heard about Misha bro, sorry bout that," Price said.

"Yeah that was messed up gang," Danno added as he went to sit back down. He hefted a Hennessy bottle. "Come have a cup bro. I know you could use one."

Tutu declined his offer. "Nall boy, I don't want no drink. I need to holla at you bro. I need a favor."

"Anything for you, Lil Tyrese," Danno said. "What you need, bro?"

Tutu started to answer, then he stopped as he looked at the unfamiliar boy sitting at the table. "No disrespect to yo guy Danno and Price, but I don't know him, so could he excuse hisself?"

"You better watch yo mouth boy, I'm gang," the boy protested. Tutu's face instantly filled with rage.

He surged forward. "Goofy, who you think you

talking to?"

Price pushed Tutu back. "He is gang, Tutu."

"Tree was gang too," Tutu snapped. "I came here to holla at my day ones, not all these new kids. Like I said, I don't know you boy, you need to move around while I holla at my guys."

"He do got a point," agreed Pooh.

Danno said, "Trell wait downstairs bro. We need to holla at our guy."

Once Danno spoke, Trell saw it was a dead issue, so he got up. "I know y'all just doing that because I was finta win the game. That's aw-ight though, leave the board just like it is."

As he left the apartment, Trell took care to avoid Tutu's eyes.

Once he was gone, Tutu asked, "Man where y'all getting these disrespectful ass shorties from? And how they don't know me? How they claiming Gray Street and ain't never even been on Gray Street?"

They all laughed.

"Facts," said Con.

"They ain't no worse than we was once upon a time," Danno observed, as he mixed up the dominos on the table. "They just want to be a part of something. I'm glad you showed though, because shorty was kicking our asses. He already up like $50 on me."

Again they laughed, but Tutu only managed to squeeze out a small chuckle.

"What's good with it though, Tutu?" asked Price.

"I need a gun. I ain't begging neither, I got bread."

"They done brought your gorilla back out, hunh?" Pooh asked. "My boy ready to turn up."

Tutu's voice shook as he said, "Man, they kilt my

girl and she was pregnant. I can't never let them live behind that."

Danno thought about it as he lit a blunt. After a bit, he said, "I felt that was what you was gone be on after I heard the news. I didn't know about the shorty though. That's really really messed up my guy. You know who it was, Tutu?"

"I don't know the shooter, but 8 Deuce Donnie was in the passenger seat of the car. I ain't have a chance to see the driver, but more than likely it was Shanno. I really could care less either way, they ass is dead. It's crackin with anybody from 8 Deuce from this day forward. I'm back in the streets putting nothing but pressure on they ass. I'm finta be a problem, boy. On God."

"You a workin man now, though," Con observed. "We ain't mad at that, but this here gone require that you turn yo savage all they way up. You ready for that?"

"Man, I'm telling you, it's bussin," Tutu replied. "How you not hearing what I'm saying?"

"Well bro, me and Con was talking earlier," Pooh said. "We said we was gone get on top of that for you. You ain't gotta get yo hands dirty. On God, bro."

"Y'all capping boy. Y'all must have forgot who I am," Tutu said with tears in his eyes. "I been out here drilling since I was a shorty. I know how to slide. Ain't no job stopped that. I was staying out the way, but they won't let me be great. Now Tutu is back. If I can't buy a banger from y'all that's cool, but I'm gone get my lick back. They girls, they kids and they mamas ain't safe. Nobody affiliated with 8 Deuce can live. I'm gone though."

"Hold on Little Tyrese," Danno said as he got to his

feet. "We ain't turning our back on you, we really want to keep you out harm's way. Boy, you been my shorty since you was like five or six. Ain't that right, Price?"

"Big facts," Price said.

Danno walked over to the couch. He and Pooh took the pillows off of it and Danno used the fabric handle to pull the bed out of the couch. As it unfolded, Tutu saw all of the guns that had been hidden inside of it.

"Look Little Tyrese, we always got you. This Danno you talking to. I'll never switch up. Now take what you want. And even if you don't want no help, we still gone be on they heels for you."

Tutu looked over the assortment of weapons. There were choppers, revolvers and semi-auto handguns, along with large capacity magazines and boxes of bullets. He didn't know what he wanted until a pretty Glock with a beam and drum clip on it caught his eye; he picked it up.

"Man, I think I want this Glizzy right here," Tutu said as he looked down the gun's sights. "How much?"

"Don't disrespect us like that, Tutu," Price said. He took the gun from Tutu and handed it to Con. "Clean and oil it up for him real quick, Con. Pooh, give him a backpack."

Pooh went to a closet and got a bag. He tossed it to Tutu, before folding the hideaway bed back into the couch and replacing the pillows. Danno put his arm around Tutu's shoulders and led him over to the card table to have a seat.

"Forget what Price said, I am gone charge you for that banger," Danno said. "I'm charging you to have a drink of this Henny with me and blow some of this weed with yo boy." Tutu shook his head as he took a seat. "I'm cool on that Henny, but I will smoke one of them blunts.

Tutu lit the blunt and sat back, letting the smoke take his mind away from his troubles for a moment. Con walked back into the room and sat the gun on the table in front of Tutu, who hefted the gun and looked at it with a wicked gleam in his eye.

"Y'all wasn't lying," Tutu said, as he aimed the gun with a blunt in the corner of his mouth. "I'm back."

CHAPTER 18

Joseph "Joe" Mission walked into the kitchen of his mother's apartment that he shared with his younger siblings and his uncle, carrying his basketball under his arm. He took a bottle of water from the fridge and opened it to take a long gulp. As he drank the cold water, he noticed Italian bread rolls on the counter and hot and mild jars of Giardiniera peppers. He looked over in the kitchen sink and saw that his mother had put a couple of buckets of Italian beef meat there to thaw.

"Yeah, yeah," he said aloud. He loved when his mom made Italian beef sandwiches, especially after coming home from a long day of school and basketball practice. He closed the refrigerator door and ran his fingers across a newspaper article taped there about him. The article was from the Sun-Times and had a split picture of him sitting in a classroom and driving to the basket during a game. The title of the article read, Phenom Student Athlete, Top Player at 16. Proudly he reread the headline for the millionth time. "That boy can score and keep a 4.0," Joe said. He made a peace sign, kissed it and touched the newspaper article. He took two granola bars from the box on top of the fridge and stuffed them in his jogging pants pocket. He left the kitchen and was on the way to let himself out the apartment, but his younger brother rushed from the bedroom they shared to stop him.

"Joe, where you going?" the 11-year old boy asked.

"I'm about to run a few drills at the park," he answered.

"I wanna go. Please, please, please."

"Not right now Josh. I'm trying to get a good run in and I don't feel like watching you. I'll take you and Josana the next time."

Josh folded his arms across his chest. "You promise?"

"Fo sho, baby bro. Joe don't lie."

"Okay, we gone be waiting. I'm gone make sure Josana is ready and she gone have on clean socks and everything."

Joe laughed. He winked at his brother as he said, "You do that. I'm not gone forget about you. I'll be back, then we can go. Now do me a favor and lock the door."

Josh did what he was asked and locked the door behind his big brother. He heard Joe skip down the stairs to the first level of the brownstone before he ran to the living room window. Through the blinds he saw Joe pull his hood on his head and put his ball down. He did a complete set of stretches before he jogged away in the direction of the nearby park.

Along the way he practiced dribbling drills as he jogged, making sure he used his weaker right hand as much as possible. Near the alley he lost his handle and the ball rolled near a garage that had seen better days. On the garage door, someone had spray painted 8 Deuce with a drawing of a thug with his hair on fire, symbolizing Hotheads. As he picked his ball up, he couldn't help but notice the artist had done a good job. He left the alley and continued on his way. The park was near, only a block away, so Joe decided to sprint the rest of the way and took off running.

By the time he reached the park's outdoor basketball court, his muscles were good and warm, though it was a bit chilly. The fieldhouse was only 100 or so feet from the outdoor court, and contained a nice court too, but Joe preferred to practice his jump shot outside. It was said that if your jump shot was pure outdoors, especially in a city as windy as Chicago, then indoors it would be straight fire.

There were a couple of kids shooting baskets on the north end of the court with a ball, Joe could tell needed some air, strictly from the way it sounded when they dribbled it. A crowd of older teenage boys were in the nearby parking lot on the side of the fieldhouse, listening to the music coming from a car parked there. He could also smell the strong acrid scent of the weed they were smoking. Joe walked to the south end of the court. It was nearest to the parking lot. He could easily hear snatches of the boys' conversation in the parking lot because they were talking above the music. It was easy to tell from what he heard and their handshakes they were 8 Deuce Hotheads. This park was considered their turf, but he wasn't worried because they usually left the athletes alone.

Before he began his shooting drills, he ran around the perimeter of the court ten times. When he was finished running, he began doing layup drills concentrating on his right hand. One of the young boys that had been playing on the other end of the court wandered down to the end where Joe was practicing.

He passed the ball to the young fella so he could take some shots, but the boy clumsily dropped the pass. As the boy chased the ball down, in a small way he reminded Joe of his little brother Josh. Right then, he wished he had brought Josh with him. He realized that he'd been so focused on working on his own game, he rarely ever took the time to help his younger brother work on his. Mentally he made a note that that would change today. Soon Joe and the younger boy worked out a system of shooting, rebounding and passing to one another. Across the parking lot, Tutu walked from behind the fieldhouse. He was wearing a black hoodie with the hood on his head. On his shoulder was slung a book bag with the zipper open. Casually he walked toward the group of 8 Deuces.

Donnie was leaning against Shanno's car arguing with another 8 Deuce named Butter about who was a better basketball player, Michael Jordan or Lebron James. Shanno and two other 8 Deuces ignored them as they smoked weed and roasted one another about their choice in girls. Shoota was in the backseat of Shanno's car passed out with a gun on his lap, and clutching an empty double cup that had once contained lean.

Tutu had cleared the shadow of the fieldhouse and was about 20 feet away from them when Butter noticed him. He tapped Donnie on the arm. Warily, he asked, "Hothead, who this walking up?"

Donnie stopped talking and squinted at the advancing figure. He tried to get a look at the face, but the stranger's hood obscured his view.

"Shanno, who that is?" Donnie asked, alerting his

friend.Shanno looked up from his conversation to see who Donnie was talking about. Tutu was about 15 feet away as he tugged the pistol from the book bag. As Shanno saw the pistol being drawn, he pulled up his sagging pants, dropped his cup of lean and took off in the direction of the basketball court. As Shanno ran past him without saying a word, Donnie didn't ask questions as he about-faced and took off after him.

Seeing two of his main opps fleeing, Tutu didn't waste a second as he began firing at them. Butter had been standing next to Donnie and he fell to the pavement as he took bullets in the neck and chest. One of the other 8 Deuces dove to the ground, and another one took off running in the opposite direction of Shanno and Donnie. Shoota never woke up and remained in the back seat. Disregarding the others, Tutu ran after them and concentrated his fire on Donnie and Shanno as they dashed across the basketball court.

Donnie and Shanno were about 50 yards away, as Tutu continued to blast at them. He saw Donnie do a little hop skip and grab his buttocks, but he kept running. Seeing that he got a hit, Tutu intensified his aim and Shanno pitched forward onto his face when a bullet whistled through his shoulder. His momentum made him roll a few times when he fell, but Shanno hurriedly got back to his feet and took off again. Tutu tried to resume firing but his gun was empty, so he watched helplessly as they made it to the street, and fled down the adjacent block.

"I'll be back!" Tutu shouted angrily. "Ain't no more outside!"

He turned to leave and looked directly into the barrel of a handgun being held by a Chicago policeman. The officer had stopped at the fieldhouse to use the bathroom and try to holler at the pretty, divorcee that ran the park, but she didn't come in today. He was digging in his pocket for change to buy a candy bar out of the vending machine in the lobby of the fieldhouse, when all hell broke loose outside. He called for backup and made his way outside in time to see Tutu emptying his clip at two boys fleeing across the park. His first instinct was to kill the shooter, but he saw that his gun was empty. Most officers wouldn't have hesitated to shoot the boy, but he would rather have a case than a body.

"Boy, I'm gone only say it once, put the gun down now or you die!" Officer Welco commanded. "If I repeat myself, you won't be around to hear it!"

Tutu dropped the gun and held up his hands.

"Get on your stomach on the ground now! Arms spread out at the side!"

Tutu complied, as he shouted, "Don't shoot! Don't shoot! I'm doing it!"

While he was on the ground, Tutu looked over at Butter, who was laying on the ground bleeding from his neck. His eyes were closed and there was a tremendous amount of blood on the ground. Officer Welco advanced cautiously to Tutu's prone body and knelt on his back. He cuffed Tutu and stood back up to use his radio.

Lying on the ground cuffed, Tutu changed the position of his head, looking in the direction of the basketball court. He saw that the group of ball players that were there when he started shooting were long gone, except for one. Joe lie face down with his eyes open, transfixed in a stare that Tutu had seen more times than he'd cared to see in his life. Officer Welco spoke urgently into his radio. "Officer on scene. I have multiple gunshot victims. I repeat multiple G.S. victims. Requesting backup and immediate medical personnel at scene. Shooter is in custody. I repeat, shooter is in custody."

On the ground, Tutu sighed loudly as he shut his eyes to block it all out and hold back the tears at the unfairness of it all.

CHAPTER 19

The Illinois Department of Corrections officer swung several sets of handcuffs and shackles as he walked back and forth in front of the row of inmates standing shoulder to shoulder in a line. The officer was broad shouldered and clean-shaven except for the bushy brown moustache that covered his thin upper lip like a brown caterpillar. The bright autumn sun reflected off the mirrored lenses of his state trooper looking sunglasses.

The line of convicted felons handcuffed and shackled in front of him wore a variety of emotions on their faces, ranging from fear, to disinterest, to anger. They were all clothed in state issued black work boots, misshapen khaki pants, ash gray crew neck sweatshirts and work jackets. The denim of their work jackets made a swishing sound whenever any of them moved.

Guarding the group of boys and men were two totally silent corrections officers carrying 12 Gauge shotguns. They also wore mirrored sunglasses and their faces showed no emotion. Behind the steering wheel of the bus they were about to board was another IDOC officer watching videos on his cell phone. He appeared to be bored at what must have been a regular routine for him.

The mustached officer stopped pacing and stopped in front of the inmates. He turned his head and spit tobacco juice. "Listen up convicts," he said in a Southern drawl. "My name is Sergeant Tanner. Not homie, or home skillet, or oh boy, or dude, or man, or bro, or gang, or whatever the hell else you call your homeboys. I am not your friend. I do not care about your guilt or innocence. I will sleep just as good in my bed if I know you're an innocent man that was given natural life. I am not your lawyer, your judge, the appeal board, your public defender or prosecutor. I am not your nanny, your mammy or your nursemaid. My job is to deliver you to the Illinois Department of Corrections facility that you have been assigned to, nothing more, nothing less." Sgt. Tanner paused to spit again. "In the event you've seen too many movies in your life and have decided that now is your time to try out your escape theory, know that Officer Kean and Officer Stewart right there will shoot you, and not stop shooting you until you are dead. Remember there is way less paperwork for a dead prisoner, than an escaped prisoner."

To emphasize Tanner's threat each officer jacked a round into their shotgun chamber with perfect timing, obviously the benefit of doing this routine countless times.

Tanner continued, "Now that we have that understanding our time together should go much smoother."

As Sgt. Tanner droned on about the rules and his love for the IDOC, Tutu drowned out his voice. He turned his face up to the sun and squinted like he'd never seen the sun before today. He could feel the chill in the October air in his bones, causing him to use his shackled hands to adjust the collar of his work jacket, and pull his skull cap down around his ears. He squinted up at the sun again, maybe hoping it would lend him some of its warmth.

Though it was mid-October it was quite chilly, but that was normal for Chicago. In the not so distant distance, Tureon could hear the growl of traffic as it snaked past the courthouse and the County jail on California Street. There were loud car horns, the screech of tires, the rumble of cars needing muffler work and every now and then the thump-thump-thump of car sounds.

On the deck in Division 10 in the County jail, the place where he'd spent the last 21 months of his life, he'd heard that once they were in one of the prisons located in Southern and Western Illinois they would miss the sounds of the city. One inmate described it as the 'loudest silence' he had ever heard. Tutu sniffed the air and could smell the strong scent of Popeye's chicken coming from the restaurant on the corner across the street from the County courthouse. It was something else he was forewarned he would miss, the city's food; he already did miss it after only 21 months.

The sights, sounds and tastes of the city was something he'd known all of his entire 19 years and now he'd be away from them for however long. Just thinking about it made his eyes grow moist as a sense of impending doom overwhelmed him. In his mind he flashed back to standing in the courtroom when the judge accepted his plea deal.

The crazy thing was, that try as he might, he couldn't

remember the name of the man that sentenced him. While it was happening, all he could hear was his heart pounding loudly in his ears. That was accompanied by a tinny taste in his mouth like he had to throw up as he stood next to his public defender. His public defender was saying something to him, but to Tutu it sounded like he was far away and he couldn't hear him. On the bench, the judge was babbling on about remorse and second chances, but his words meant less than nothing to Tutu. As the judge was about to announce his sentence, two Cook County sheriffs stepped up behind him to get ready to take him into custody. As they put their hands on his shoulders, Tutu looked over his shoulder into the courtroom audience. There wasn't a single member of the Gray Street Gang, from his affiliation in attendance; not one. His mother was there and he could tell from the glassy look in her eyes that she was drunk even though it was only ten in the morning. They locked eyes and she mouthed, "I love you." Though he loved her, he just couldn't say it back, instead he nodded before turning back to the judge. The judge was finally wrapping up his lengthy speech by asking, "Do you have anything to say on your behalf, Mr. Young?"

Tutu thought about it for a moment, then simply shook his head. In his mind, it wouldn't change anything, no matter what he said, so he decided not to waste his breath. The judge handed down his 60 year sentence without ceremony, which was no surprise to Tutu. The sheriffs took him into custody without incident and deposited him into one of the bullpens behind the courtrooms to await transportation back to his deck in the jail.

He sat quietly listening to the other inmates in the bullpen talk amongst themselves. Some of them had been sentenced today and were in pretty good spirits. Instead of going to prison, some of them were acting like they'd been given an island vacation. They were talking about all the movement, the better food, and the housing in the penitentiary like they were going to a resort compared to the deplorable, crowded conditions of the Cook County jail. As soon as the last prisoner came from court, the excited inmates were lined up and taken back to their housing.

During the next week as Tutu awaited transportation to the prison he would be assigned to, he could barely sleep or eat. Thursday he was summoned to receive his state issue prison wardrobe and told to pack up his belongings to leave the following morning. After that he had to rush back to his cell to use the toilet because he had the bubble guts.

He didn't sleep a wink that night, so he was dressed and ready to go long before the deputies came around to get him. Tutu left behind a few toiletries and food items to his cellmate because he was pretty cool. Once he left the deck, things were a blur and shortly afterwards he was handcuffed and shackled with other inmates. They hobble-walked outside the jail to the bus that would transport them downstate to the Northern Reception and Classification Center or NRC at the old Stateville Penitentiary for intake. The men and boys that were on their way to prison for the first time would be in intake longer than the prisoners that had been to prison before.

As they stood in the chilly, early morning air with the sun barely in the sky, a mixture of fear of the unknown and sadness at his plight played with Tutu's emotions. He forced himself to bring his mind back to the present, so he could make sure he didn't make a mistake. In the County jail, not paying attention to the sheriff's deputies' instructions could earn you a quick, but ruthless beating. He had seen the deputies send several inmates to the hospital for not listening and following instructions, and in his mind he knew the IDOC officers wouldn't be any different.

"...and now if you convicts will climb aboard in an orderly manner, we can be on our merry way," Sgt. Tanner drawled.

One by one each inmate stepped forward and had their ID wristbands scanned before climbing onto the bus. Each man chose a seat and sat down. Soon the bus was loaded and they were on their way after making it through several checkpoints to leave the jail. As they drove through the city headed for the highway, the inmates began to talk amongst themselves, quietly at first, but they grew louder and more animated as they looked out of the bus windows. They talked about how much they would miss some of the restaurants and places they saw along the way to the expressway. While they were talking about food, Tutu was trying his best not to be sick to his stomach from an anxiety attack.

As the bus made it to the expressway entrance, Tutu looked across the aisle at the inmate with his eyes closed and laid back against the seat, chilling like he was on his way to work or someplace other than prison. He was a huge, bear of a man that sported a full beard and a bald head.

The excited chatter about landmarks, food and

women still flowed from the back of the bus, but Tureon wasn't listening. He couldn't think about any of that right now. All he could think about was that he was about to leave behind everything he'd ever known for what may be the rest of his life. He closed his eyes to try and calm himself, but all he could see was Misha's lifeless eyes, his mother's tired, bloodshot eyes, and his aunt's disappointed eyes.

Though it was the morning rush hour in Chicago, traffic in the southbound lanes of the expressway were moving swiftly and soon they were on the outskirts of the city. The scenery outside the bus was a blur as tears began to free themselves from Tutu's eyes and cascade down his face. He thought his weeping was going unnoticed until the older prisoner behind him started kicking his seat.

"Don't cry now, little killer," he stage-whispered. "You a savage. You a real one. I swear I don't care. Dry them tears now little negaro, you wasn't cryning when you did what you did. You was a big bad boy out there with a gun. Be big and bad in here where there ain't no guns."

The inmate laughed heartily at his own words while Tutu tried to ignore him as he wiped his tears.

"Savage, savage, savage, about tough as some cabbage," chanted the obviously insane man. "Savage, savage, savage, shooters need to practice. Savage, savage, savage…"

The inmate across the aisle from Tutu opened his eyes for the first time in miles. He turned and looked at the inmate behind Tutu boring holes into him with his intense maroon eyes.

"Aye man be quiet," he commanded in a deep voice

that matched his size. "Milo, show some respect Black man. Stop kicking little homie's chair and chill out. Don't nobody want to hear that mess. Them white folks done already judged him and now you gone judge him too hunh? Act like you been to the joint before and let that man do his own time."

The mentally challenged Milo used one of his handcuffed hands to cover his mouth, but they could still hear him chanting though it was muffled now. A couple of the other inmates laughed, but not too loudly seemingly out of respect for the inmate that had spoken to Milo. None of it really mattered to Tutu as he sadly leaned his head against the window and sniffled several times as quietly as possible. The inmate across the aisle from him returned to his relaxed state, sitting back with his eyes closed.

Without opening his eyes, the huge inmate across the aisle said, "You know what little homie? His old crazy ass is right, ain't no times for tears now, you here now. And don't let none of these dudes on this bus fool you neither, everybody done cried they tears. If they ain't as scared as you now, they was they first time going to the joint. You from the city?"

"Yeah, Southside," Tutu answered miserably. "Gray Street."

"Okay little homie, Southside, that's wassup. They call me O.G."

"Tutu," he replied.

"Well like I said Tutu, you here now. You got to make the best of it. I ain't trying to be your best friend, but I feel like I should tell you like somebody told me on my first bit. If you were out there doing bad things what did you expect to happen? Now if you're an innocent man that's another story, but the fact of the matter is only you and God know the answer to that question."

An inmate several rows in front of them yelled, "That sound like me O.G., I'm innocent."

"Yeah that's what I was trying to tell them people," said another inmate. "As pure and innocent as freshly fallen snow."

O.G. laughed good and hard at that one. "Stop it Monko, you can't even spell innocent."

Monko screwed up his brown face in thought before he said aloud, "Innocent. N-o-sent. Innocent." Even Tutu had to smile at Monko's terrible attempt.

"My point exactly," O.G. said with a grin, though his eyes remained closed. Once again his voice turned serious as he said, "Tutu, I been down a coupla times little homie, I mean we all make mistakes. I ain't never been locked up for the same thing twice though. I know you feeling a way over there, but what you gotta do is think about what you did to get you here, and when you get out, make sure you don't do it again."

Tutu may not have appeared to be listening to O.G., but he'd heard every word, though he couldn't bring himself to admit that he wasn't getting out for a long time, if ever. His tears fell faster and harder as he leaned his head back against the window and watched the countryside pass by.

THE END.

CHAPTER 1 DISCUSSION QUESTIONS

1. Have you ever been filled with fear from something you saw happen to a loved one or even a stranger? Was your response similar or different from Tutu's?

2. Have you ever rejected or taken advice from an elder that proved beneficial to you?

3. Have you ever had to deliver bad news to a loved one or someone? How did you do so, in person or over the phone? Was their reaction one that you expected or not? How so?

4. Have you ever witnessed something as a kid that you feel changed your life?

CHAPTER 2 DISCUSSION QUESTIONS

1. What do you believe makes a "deadbeat" or "unfit" parent? What do you think could be done to get rid of that label once it has been put upon someone?

2. Is there such a thing as funeral etiquette? If so, describe it.

3. Do you think a parent should be kept away from their children by the other parent? Why or why not?

4. Should negative life events be recorded by others or should people step up to help solve problems that they see? Why or why not? Compare and contrast snitching and informing?

5. Should revenge be sought after even if it will not change anything? How else can people make themselves feel better about a tragedy concerning a loved one?

CHAPTER 3 DISCUSSION QUESTIONS

1. What is it that you own that makes you feel naked if you do not have it with you? How do you define

security? Do you think there is a difference and/or similarity between hunting an animal and killing a person? How so?

2. What are some things that you do to make the heartache of losing a loved one go away?

3. Why do you think getting an education is undervalued or "boring" to many teens?

4. Do you think public memorials do more harm than good or vice versa? Why or why not?

CHAPTER 4 DISCUSSION QUESTIONS

1. Do you think marijuana should be smoked by teenagers?

2. Have you ever wanted to leave a situation, but did not want to be teased by friends for leaving?

3. Have you ever been tricked into a situation that you did not want to be in? What did/could you learn from that experience?

4. Do you think being suspended from school makes someone a better or worse student?

CHAPTER 5 DISCUSSION QUESTIONS

1. If you were the parent of a high schooler, would you care if they were suspended and then made to stay home from school?

2. In your opinion, does social media have a positive or negative impact on teens and/or young adults and how they deal with conflict? How so?

3. Many boys approach girls disrespectfully in today's society, why is that?

4. Why do you think a natural response for some males to rejection from a girl is to hit her?

CHAPTER 6 DISCUSSION QUESTIONS

1. Do you think teenagers should be given a curfew by their parents or the government? In your opinion, are curfews helpful or a good thing?

2. Do you think that alcohol and drugs like marijuana are helpful or a hindrance to adolescent growth?

3. As a young adult or teenager, how do you think it feels to have to always be aware and prepared to defend yourself at all times?

4. When it comes to friendships, if you notice the ways of a friend that prove to be dangerous or full of drama, should you continue the friendship or end it?

CHAPTER 7 DISCUSSION QUESTIONS

1. Do you think older people, our elders, still have a role in the lives of young people? Why or why not?

2. What does spirituality/religion mean to you?

3. Do you have faith in something? If so explain where your faith lies.

4. What do you think the caring lady "knew" as she walked away from the ambulance hugging herself?

CHAPTER 8 DISCUSSION QUESTIONS

1. What do you think Tutu's rap lyrics were about that he wrote while in the hospital? If you were him, what would your lyrics be about?

2. Do you think Tutu really wants a school lunchroom burger, a return to childhood, or a normal teen life?

3. What does it mean to you to have a friend or to be a friend to someone?

4. Should a parent do more than provide food, shelter, and clothing for their children?

5. What role do you think a father should play in the life and raising of his son vs. his daughter?

CHAPTER 9 DISCUSSION QUESTIONS

1. Should dealing with rejection be something that is taught in the home amongst family members?
2. How does greed factor into cause and effect outcomes?
3. What should the role of Black men be in younger men/boys lives if they are a part of the same family?
4. Do you think a man should protect a woman against another man that is seemingly a threat?
5. Why do you think gun violence has almost become an automatic response to a threat instead of a fist fight?
6. Do you have a safe place in your life that you go to during troubling times? If not, would you want one?

CHAPTER 10 DISCUSSION QUESTIONS

1. If practicing is not valuable, then how do people get better at doing something?
2. Is it easy or hard to give a friend constructive criticism?
3. Why do rap diss records start or continue street wars if it's only music?
4. What makes someone jealous of another person, or even a friend?
5. How could you show care and loyalty to a friend that feels like you've wronged them?
6. Do you agree or disagree with the belief that "success brings the best and worst out of the people closest to you"?

CHAPTER 11 DISCUSSION QUESTIONS

1. How do you think it would feel to love doing something, but being hated for doing it?

2. Why do you think Geno told Tutu, "Make music, not memes?

3. Do you think that Tree should apologize to Tutu for his tantrum, jealousy, or distance?

4. Do you know of anyone with the same type of negative attitude as Tree? If so do you like or dislike being around them?

5. Since he'd gotten shot, Tutu rarely went anywhere without a gun. Do you think you get into more trouble carrying a gun all the time?

CHAPTER 12 DISCUSSION QUESTIONS

1. Is Tree a "snitch" or just protecting himself from jail time?

2. Who was more loyal to their friendship at the police station, Tree or Tutu?

3. Do you think the policeman's tactics are underhanded or unfair?

4. Tutu seems to have accepted his fate of being locked up, do you think that's an easy thing to do?

CHAPTER 13 DISCUSSION QUESTIONS

1. Do you think Tutu matured any during the time he was in jail?

2. Does it seem like having certain types of friends while you're locked up can get you into more or less trouble? Give an example of positive and negative types of friends.

3. Do you think spending months and years away from family and loved ones can change a person permanently?

4. Upon being released from jail or prison after serving time, do you think a person has learned their lessons most times, or do they return to their old ways?

5. Mr. Kindle, the counselor, offered Tutu mentorship outside of jail, do you think that's needed? Or is it unnecessary?

CHAPTER 14 DISCUSSION QUESTIONS

1. Tutu's girlfriend, Misha, knew her friend set him up to be shot, do you think she should tell him? If yes, why? If no, why?

2. What are some of the things that changed while Tutu was locked up?

3. Do you think the threat of being targeted by the opps (enemies) is what stops many youth from going to school and/or seeking jobs?

4. Tutu has stopped smoking weed, do you think that allows him to make better decisions?

5. Do you think drug use and abuse plays a huge role in the gang culture?

CHAPTER 15 DISCUSSION QUESTIONS

1. In real life, do you think it's hard to go from being a street guy to getting a job?

2. Things like working your first job are often harder in your mind than in actuality. Name something you've done that turned out to be much easier and more enjoyable than you thought it would be in the beginning.

TO LIVE & DIE IN CHIRAQ

3. Though Tutu wasn't gang banging at the time, things quickly took a turn for the worst, do you understand how that happened?

4. Shoota's character represents all young boys that are ordered to participate in crimes by older gang members. Is he misled?

5. Is Misha an innocent victim or does she deserve to be shot because her boyfriend is a gang member?

CHAPTER 16 DISCUSSION QUESTIONS

1. Should Misha's grandmother have been angry with Tutu?

2. Why wasn't her brother angry with him also?

3. Do you think someone ever fully recovers from such a great loss?

4. Though many families rarely seek therapy after such a tragedy, do you think it would help them?

CHAPTER 17 DISCUSSION QUESTIONS

1. After the death of his girlfriend and unborn child, Tutu is walking around with a huge chip on his shoulder, is that dangerous?

2. In a short amount of time, new gang members don't know who Tutu is or what's he's done for the gang in the past, why does that make him so mad?

3. Tutu is willing to take revenge on anyone, is that wrong?

4. Tutu feels he has no other path but the one he's headed down, is that true or false?

CHAPTER 18 DISCUSSION QUESTIONS

1. Are the members of the 8 Deuce Hotheads wrong for hanging out in the park around civilians when they have so many enemies?

2. In some small way is it Joe's fault he was killed because he chose to stay at the court and shoot baskets so close to gang bangers?

3. Do you notice how the cycle continues now that Joe is killed, his little brother has to grow up without him because he was a victim of gun violence?

4. Do you think Tutu evens the score with his act of vengeance?

CHAPTER 19 DISCUSSION QUESTIONS

1. Does it seem unfair that Tutu is the one going to prison for trying to avenge the murders of his girlfriend and unborn child?

2. Can you see how cause-and-effect has led Tutu up to this moment?

3. The judge sentenced him to 60 years. Was that too long or too short a sentence for his crime?

4. None of the members of his gang from Gray Street were there when he was sentenced, should he have been hurt by that?

5. What do you think about the advice OG offered Tutu on the prison bus?